D1827528

ALL OUT

ALL OUT

A NOVEL BY JUDITH ALGUIRE

New Victoria Publishers, Inc.
A Feminist Literary and Cultural Organization

Copyright © 1988, by Judith Alguire
All rights reserved.

Published by New Victoria Publishers.
PO Box 27 Norwich, Vermont 05055

Library of Congress Number 88-061510

ISBN 0-934678-16-2

To my animal friends, especially to Sally, Barnie, Betsy, Chumbly, Mrs. Marvel, Tomahawk and Prince.

Chapter One

"Kay."

Kay glanced up to see Bill Bordeaux standing in front of the counter. She looked at him over her glasses. From her elevated position in the dispensary, Bill looked shorter and slighter than usual. Bill Bordeaux—years removed from Shawinigan Falls. If you listened carefully, you might catch a trace of La Belle Provence but it was very slight. Kay sometimes regretted that he had been swallowed up in the greatest Francophobic city in the world.

Sometimes, when he had just returned from a visit home, the accent would be a little heavier—but just a touch—and he would be more animated. He would move one hand when he spoke and she would say: "Bill, you've been visiting 'The Falls' again." And he would nod and give her a sheepish little smile.

At times like that, she could see him stepping onto the ice for the old Montreal Canadiens. Right now, standing before her as pale and perfect as if poured from wax, he looked for all the world like a Bay Street accountant.

Bill Bordeaux had been her coach since her freshman year at the University of Toronto. Years ago he had led the Boston Marathon until the twenty-three mile mark, but he had 'hit the wall' of energy depletion, and collapsed in the street. Nothing like that had ever happened to anyone he coached, he would tell her ruefully.

1

Kay took her glasses off and lay them aside. "Bill, what brings you to this part of town?"

"Do you have a minute? Can we go somewhere to talk?"

"I can't leave the store. Come on up." She pushed open the door to her cubbyhole. "Cozy, isn't it? I've even got some coffee brewing. Do you want the chair or would you care to sit on a box of Penicillin?"

Bill sat down and accepted the coffee which she poured into a Styrofoam cup.

She continued, "I'm sticking to my training schedule exactly as you wrote it. I'm not fooling around. I'm not doing anything crazy. I'll bet you're here to check up on me."

The coffee was bitter but Bill drank it anyway. "You make me think I should be checking on you. We'll go over your training schedule in detail on Sunday. I want to see everything you've written down. You have written everything down?"

"I've written everything down."

"Good. That's not what I've come to talk to you about though."

"Shoot."

"It's about the dinner Saturday."

"You don't need to worry. I said I would come and I will."

"I trust you to do what you say you will. It's about Debbie."

"Debbie's coming too."

"I know that." Bill sighed audibly. "I don't like to ask this, but I want you to have a word with Debbie. I want you to make sure that she comes to this shindig looking respectable."

Kay looked at the coach sharply. "Who have you been talking to? This isn't you."

"I don't care to say," he said unhappily. "Some people are cringing. They're afraid she's going to show up in that jean jacket with all those buttons plastered over it."

"The ones that say: Mother Nature is a Lesbian?"

2

"Yes, that sort of thing." Bill paused and drained the Styrofoam cup stoically. "There will be a lot of important people there. If we make a good impression it could make a big difference in our future funding. That's going to be important to a lot of kids."

Kay looked at Bill, exasperated. "Why me? Why do I get to do the dirty work? What am I getting out of this? I don't take a cent from the Fund. I wouldn't take a cent from the Fund if Otto Jelinek pushed it from Ottawa to Toronto with his nose. Why do you think I work here. For my health?"

Bill stared for a moment at the crisp white lab coat. The name tag said: Kay Strachan, Pharmacist. It should have said: Kay Strachan, Marathon Runner. The job at Pop's paid the bills and bought the custom-made running shoes. It also took up time and used up energy. Bill resented the demands that Pop's made on Kay's time. But what options were there for an athlete too stubborn to seek endorsements and too proud to accept charity from the Olympic Fund? "You're on the team, Kay," he said simply.

"If I do my thing in Ottawa, I'm on the team. The jerks won't even give me a preselection."

"You're going to be on the team."

"I won Boston last year," Kay continued, unmollified. "I set a world record and I still have to place in the National Capital to qualify. That's nuts, Bill."

"I know it's nuts but that's the system." His voice pleaded. "Will you talk to Deb?"

"No matter what I say, it will be either the jean jacket or the three-piece suit with the tie and stickpin."

"Jesus!"

"The woman would look dumb in chiffon. Whipper Billy Watson would drool over her muscles. She looks OK in the three-piece suit."

3

"Do you think we could get rid of the tie and vest?" he ventured hopefully. "The buttons too. They've got to go. That's the worst part."

"I hate the idea of approaching her on this."

"We've all got to make sacrifices."

"What sacrifices have you made, Bill?"

"I tore my hair out," he said, unperturbed. "What I didn't tear out turned grey. I grew an ulcer convincing a stubborn kid that she wasn't medal material in the middle distances. I've coached you for free since you left U of T."

"Sorry." Kay shook her head, mildly chastened. "It just sticks in my craw, seeing you buckle under so a bunch of fat cats won't be offended. It isn't like you."

Bill smiled. "I've learned to adjust to a lot of things over the years. I've learned to compromise. There are always things that go against the grain. First it was boys with long hair. Then it was the discipline problems. You have to work awfully hard to win an athlete's respect now. I've adjusted to a lot of things."

"The boys wearing earrings. The girls liking the girls," Kay said impishly.

"A lot of things, because I love to work with athletes."

"Because you still believe in the Olympic ideal. You still think that you might find your Pheidippides*. I love you for that, Guillaume." Kay regarded Bill with affectionate merriment and, for a moment, Bill was afraid that she was going to hug him.

"Don't get fresh with me now," he said stuffily. "Nobody but my priest calls me Guillaume and he's dead."

* Pheidippides—Greek messenger who ran from Marathon to Athens in 490 BC to bring the Greeks news of the victory over the Persians, and died from the effort. The distance of the modern matathon equals the distance between Marathon and Athens (26.2 miles)

4

* * *

"I think it's disgusting," Tab said when Kay informed her of Bill's mission. "I don't know how you could agree to such a thing."

"I owe Bill. I feel worse for him having to ask than I do for me having to do it. Besides, he's just asking her to give up her buttons for one evening."

"He's asking her to pretend she's something she isn't," said Tab, disgusted. "Why must women always compromise themselves that way? You should be ashamed. I hope, at the very least, that you'll handle the situation tactfully."

"I'm sure they'd be happier if she didn't show up at all. At least nobody suggested that she stay away."

"That's very big of them! She's only the best shot-putter this country has ever produced. What are you going to say to her ?"

"I'm not sure." Kay flipped the television to the sports channel. Bob MacLean was vilifying the Leafs again.

She turned the television off. "I thought I'd go to her place to pick her up for the reception. If she's wearing the jean jacket, I'll tell her how much I like the suit. If she puts on the tie, I'll tell her how much better she looks with an open neck. If she puts on any of the buttons, I may have to be frank."

"You're courage personified."

"Maybe." Kay stared at the wall. She felt very tired all of a sudden. "I think I'm getting out of Pop's later every night. I used to be locked up and out of there by nine-fifteen. Tonight, I thought I'd lost a tray of Demerol. I spent half an hour looking for it. As it turned out, I'd miscounted in the first place. What time was it when I got home, Tab?"

"I didn't look."

"I swear, I have less and less time for myself every day."

"You have all day Sunday."

"I have to go over my training schedule with Bill." Kay

5

turned the television on again. On the television, Bob was showing basketball clips.

"That won't take long."

"It may take all afternoon. He's broken up with Helen. He won't have anywhere else to go."

"Is he upset?"

"I don't know. He didn't say anything to me. He told Terry Kilroy. Man talk, you know. Terry was in Pop's around eight. He came all the way downtown to buy safes. He said he wanted to remind me of what I'm missing."

"Terry's disgusting."

"I know, but he's a good training partner on the long runs. When he moved up to the long distances I thought he might become a eunuch. Most of them do."

"But not Terry."

Kay shook her head. "He bought three boxes of extra-large. I offered to sell him a garter belt to hold them up."

"I suppose he had a brilliant rejoinder to that."

"I don't care to repeat it."

Caesar, the cat, entered the room and slowly circled Tab's legs. Tab picked him up and put him in her lap. He lay draped across her knees like a large orange caterpillar. "What happened between Bill and Helen?"

"Helen wanted to move in with him. I guess she got tired of living out in Pickering and having Bill drop in for his weekly visits. Bill told Terry that living together is against his religion. He's a good Catholic. He thinks that, in the eyes of God, he would be living in sin."

"What does he think he's doing now?"

"I guess he figures God's too busy to notice a quick fuck on Sundays."

"It's amazing how men think."

"I don't care to think about how men think." Bob had

6

switched from the NBA to a track event in Houston. Mary Decker floated across the screen in eerie splendour. "I feel tired this week, Tab. I really need a good rest on Sunday."

"Don't forget, we're going to Mother's for dinner."

"Shit!"

"It's her first dinner in her new house."

"Anyone who would leave a nice apartment downtown to move to North York has to be out of her mind."

"She wanted to have a house again."

"North York is the ugliest city in the world."

"Sudbury is the ugliest city in the world."

"OK, North York is the second ugliest city in the world." Kay paused to watch Mary Decker on the straight away. "I'd like to lose two pounds," she murmured. "If I lost two pounds, I'd be one hundred per cent where I want to be."

"So, lose two pounds."

"Bill doesn't want me to. He thinks I'm already too lean. I'm going to have another test done. I'm sure I need to squeeze out a couple of pounds."

Mary Decker disappeared into a commercial. Kay turned the television off and sat back with a sigh, saying, "Problems. Sometimes I think I have nothing but problems. If I go over there and tell Debbie how nice the suit looks, she'll probably think I'm putting the make on her. She'll spend the rest of the evening patting my rear end."

"Tell her that you don't want her to pat your rear end," said Tab patiently. "Educate the woman, Kay. Explain to her that your body is personal territory."

"Yeah." Kay stood up, stretching wearily. "Louise told her not to pat her rear end once. Debbie grabbed her breast instead. Louise's lucky. She can bench press two hundred pounds."

"I think you should help her." Tab curled Caesar into a comfortable ball. "Debbie's a big woman. She's responding to a

7

heterosexual stereotype that says big gay women are supposed to be macho."

"She's a regular diesel-dyke, Tab."

"I think you and Louise encourage her advances. They pump up your already gigantic egos."

"I'm too tired to get into that one." Kay turned toward the bathroom. "Are you going to bed soon?"

"I've got to mark a few more papers." Tab reached for her briefcase and took out a stack of papers. She picked up a pencil and started to leaf through them, leaning awkwardly over Caesar to use the arm of the chair as a desk.

Kay stood in the doorway of the bathroom, squeezing toothpaste onto her brush. "Why don't you put the cat down?"

"I just brought him up."

"OK."

Tab wrinkled her forehead, signalling herself to concentrate on her work. She scanned each paper quickly, circling spelling errors, highlighting grammatical errors with dramatic exclamation marks. With that out of the way, she hoped to be more objective about the contents of the compositions.

Water gushed noisily from the faucets and gurgled happily along the drain pipes. Tab assumed that Kay was brushing her teeth. She continued to make her stabs and dashes against the background of running water.

The water stopped. Tab paused in her work to listen to Kay undressing. She could hear the clothes drop softly into the hampers that she, Tab, had labelled: WHITE, COLOURED, FILTHY. There were brief pauses as the clothes dropped. Kay, Tab knew, couldn't resist admiring her body in front of the mirror.

When Kay came out of the bathroom, she found Tab exactly as she had left her, in the same awkward position, leaning on one elbow, staring hard at the papers in front of her. Caesar

8

lay on her lap, stretching and flexing his claws against her thigh.

Kay went into the bedroom. She pulled back the covers and got into Tab's bed naked. Tab had been doing the laundry again. The sheets felt cool and fresh against her skin. It was pleasant to lie there and stretch her sore muscles and listen to Tab sigh and grumble over her papers. If Tab finished her work soon, Kay thought hopefully, she could ask for a massage.

When Tab came to bed, it was after one. Kay was asleep, lying on her back, arms stretched over her head. Her fists were clenched and her face looked tense. Tab studied her gravely. The expression, she thought, was the same one she had seen on Kay's face that day at Boston four years ago. Kay had paced herself improperly, had run into cramps on Heartbreak Hill and straggled over the finish line placing a disappointing eighth. Kay still refused to discuss her first Boston Marathon.

Tab dumped Caesar onto the bed. He curled up on Kay's chest and started to purr. Kay didn't move a muscle.

Chapter Two

"Why did we do this?"

Kay stirred drowsily on her pillow. "Do what?"

"Make love tonight."

"Because I wanted to be close to somebody." Kay opened her eyes then closed them again. She wasn't in the mood for soul-searching.

"You can be close to me without having sex."

"When I get close to you, I want to have sex." Kay propped herself up on one elbow and tweaked Tab's cheek mischievously." All those years in track paid off. You've kept your body."

"For me, it's ideology. For you, it's convenience. You're too lazy to go out and find another great body."

"I know, I know." Kay's lips curved into a smile. "You gave yourself to me because I was a sister in need."

"I didn't give myself to you. I shared my body with you. That's an important distinction."

Kay started to laugh. "Is that the latest buzz-word of that group of yours? Sharing bodies?" She dropped back onto the bed, shaking her head. "Now I feel as if I've just participated in the Last Supper."

"Sharing is important if women are to be truly liberated," Tab continued patiently. "By making ourselves available to each other sexually, we can remove what is really a very basic human need from the arenas of power struggle and emotional

10

blackmail. Sex can be a valid function of friendship, Kay, quite divorced from the property nature of exclusive sex-centered relationships."

Kay laughed. "You're making sex sound like a duty." She turned onto her back, stretching her arms over her head. "Well, I didn't get the feeling that you were performing a social service for me just now," she said smugly. "I thought you were pretty hot."

"My beliefs don't preclude passion," said Tab primly.

"Oh, ho." Kay started to giggle. "Passion! Last week, you told me that you were going through a stage of sexual calm. I thought you—the whole group—had eschewed sex in order to achieve psychic calm. See," she said triumphantly, "I do listen to what you say."

"We didn't make a pact, binding ourselves to celibacy. You weren't listening after all. The point of the discussion was choice. Tonight, I felt aroused. I made a conscious choice to go with the feeling."

"You used to be so predictable," Kay sighed. "Your pattern of sexual arousal made the calendar virtually obsolete. Monday—start getting twitchy; Tuesday—eat a lot of grapefruit; Wednesday—stare into space and cross legs a lot. Tonight, you were ready to make it with the kitchen table and I didn't see any of the preliminary signs."

"You're indecent. Sometimes I think you're worse than Terry Kilroy. If you were a man, I couldn't tolerate it in you."

Kay frowned. "If I were a man, I couldn't tolerate it in me. So, what got you going tonight? Surely it wasn't this tired old body. Did some gorgeous woman pass by your window? Is that what set you off?"

"Your emphasis on the physical is very hard to handle sometimes," Tab said resignedly. "If I didn't know you better, I'd suspect that you view women as little more than sex ob-

11

jects." She dropped her head back onto the pillow and stared at the ceiling for a long time. "I met a woman today," she said finally. "I was sitting in the corner of the faculty lounge, reading a book...."

"Instant chemistry?"

Tab ignored Kay's remark. "She's a new professor in Women's Studies. She's particularly interested in the influence of language on the status of women. I invited her to our next meeting."

"So, what does she look like?"

"That's not important."

"Let me guess. She's built like a brick outhouse and dresses like Golda Meir. That's what got your juices flowing."

"I think she's very attractive." Tab's expression sobered Kay immediately.

"Appearance is very subjective of course," Tab continued. "It's not uncommon to find someone very attractive only to discover that no one else does. Objectively? She's very tall and has glossy black curls falling to her shoulders." Tab looked at Kay pleadingly. "I suppose there was some chemistry."

Kay smiled. This time she wasn't teasing. "In four or five months, I'm going to envy the way you feel right now," she said softly. "But at this stage of the game, I can't afford it. Love is like a drug. It makes you feel you're on top of the world when your performance is lousy. I hope this thing isn't contagious. I haven't been out looking. I'd hate to catch it at home."

"Her name is Esther."

"Bring her over. I'd like to meet her."

"I think I'll wait, thanks. I don't want to have to explain you right away, Kay."

"I thought you liberated women didn't have to explain that sort of thing to anyone. Who you're sleeping with, I mean."

"I don't have to explain to her that we sleep together occasionally. What I need to prepare her for is a macho jock with a foul mouth."

"Tab, I'll keep my mouth shut and do needlepoint."

"I want to get to know her better—on an intellectual level—before I invite her here."

"Is it because we have only one bedroom? I can make sure I'm out."

"We're having lunch tomorrow. She's interested in my notes on matriarchal societies."

"I don't know if I can stand another person who's interested in matriarchal societies. Does she hate her mother too?"

"I don't hate my mother, Kay. My interest in matriarchal societies is not a reaction to my mother. It's a natural outcome of my involvement in the feminist community. I have never hated my mother. What I hate is the fact that she named me Tabatha. Why a woman whose surname is Hunter would call her child Tabatha is beyond me."

"You should be thankful she didn't call you Catfish."

Tab did not respond.

"Well, I wish you luck," Kay said finally. She reached over to stroke Tab's hair. It was short and thick and silvery-blonde and she loved to touch it. "If you like her, I hope something develops. I know how you love to have romance in your life." She rolled over so she was facing Tab. "Remember how we thought we were in love just after I moved in with you?" She shook her head, laughing. "It was so funny. We'd been friends for at least six years. We must have shared a shower a million times. Then, all of a sudden, we were twitchy and nervous. And we made love and, just before we did, you could have cut the tension with a knife. We got very romantic and then we both started laughing. We knew that we'd known each other too long to pull off that kind of bullshit."

"I was happy when we started laughing."

13

"Yeah." Kay stared hard into the blue eyes for a moment, then she smiled. "You know what I like so much about making love to you?"

"You don't have to send me flowers."

"No," Kay said, shaking her head, "it's not because I don't have to send you flowers. It's because I like you so much. Because it's fun. Because I don't have to worry about doing something wrong." She rolled onto her back, folding her arms behind her head. "You know," she said seriously, "it's hard going to bed with a new woman."

"You try too hard, Kay. You feel obliged to give every woman a blinding orgasm. It's part of your macho makeup."

"I don't like the feeling of being out of control. It's scary, Tab."

"That's part of your macho makeup too."

"No it's not." Kay paused, biting at her lip pensively. "Nobody likes being out of control. With you, I know what's going to happen. Even if I don't know, I know it's going to be all right. I'll feel the same way about myself when it's over and I'll feel the same way about you."

"You're afraid of change." Tab looked over at her friend. Kay was staring at the wall now and she looked far away. "Remember how much trouble Bill had convincing you to do your long runs in the country? He thought you were getting stale and needed a change. You were so enamoured of the route you'd worked out. You knew the exact distances between buildings, the exact slope of each hill, which parts of the course you had to work hard on, and where you could coast on the downhill sections. You feel the same way about the Kleinburg route now. Persuading you to change is like trying to pry a teddy bear from a baby."

"All athletes are like that. Athletes like routine."

"Well, this fetish for routine is spilling over into the rest of

14

your life." Tab shook her head. "I'm worried about what will happen to you when I go to North Borneo for my field work. You'll live like a clam."

Kay didn't respond for a moment. Caesar loped over the side of the bed and settled himself between Kay and Tab. His shaggy, fat body easily occupied a third of the bed. Kay patted him absently. "I wish you had gone out for the sixty metres instead of the hurdles," she said finally. "If you had concentrated on the sixty metres, you might be going to the Olympics with me. You were a lousy hurdler."

"I liked the hurdles. It meant more to me to be a lousy hurdler than a great sprinter." Tab paused. "I never considered sports to be a career anyway. Track was something fun to do in university. I'm not sure if sports are relevant."

"Relevant to who?" Kay could tell by Tab's expression that she was preparing to make a speech.

"To the world. Perhaps, particularly, to the women's movement. What do sports really do to advance women? As far as I can tell, they benefit only the elite, those few women at the top, particularly those who fit the male notion of what a female athlete should look like. You know what I mean, Kay. Look at the way women are made up for the tennis calendars. Look at the athletes selected for that Sport swimsuit issue. These are elite athletes. These are strong women, the women we hoped would serve as role models for the next generation. What we have instead are women adhering slavishly to male attitudes about what women should be, what they should look like and who they should sleep with. Do you think that Jan Stephensen gets all those endorsements because she's a better golfer than...?" Tab paused then, with a sigh, said, "Besides, and perhaps more to the point, sports foster competition rather than cooperation. Cooperation is the key to advancement."

"Not if you're aiming for a sub 2:19 marathon." Kay turned

over onto her side so that she was facing in the opposite direction and pretended that she was falling asleep. Caesar, mildly miffed, rearranged himself behind her knees.

Tab turned on her pillow, propping herself up with one elbow. She knew that Kay would be asleep within minutes. She watched her, frowning slightly, as the breathing became gradually slower, deeper and more regular.

Kay 'The Bishop' Strachan—a classmate with a fondness for Upper Canadian history had given her that nickname in high school and it had stuck. Tab dropped back to her pillow with a sigh. She had known Kay since their freshman year on the University of Toronto track team. That was almost ten years ago now.

Tab remembered Kay at eighteen as a vivacious, dark-haired, dark-eyed girl with a permanent tan. Although she made no effort to ingratiate herself to anyone, everyone wanted to be her friend. For some reason, Kay had chosen her, Tab, and later had allowed Louise Patterson and Debbie Spencer to join the select inner circle.

Now, ten years later, Kay was a striking woman. The baby fat had disappeared into the ultra leanness of a world-class marathoner. Indeed, she was so thin now that her ribs showed and every muscle in her body stood out in extreme definition. She had the startling spectral appearance of a greyhound. The thinness made her face taut too, accentuated the cheekbones and sometimes made her look sad.

As a freshman, Tab hadn't taken her seriously when Kay told her that she had decided to become a pharmacist because she wanted a career that wouldn't interfere with running. She, Tab, had selected the school of anthropology with great care. At seventeen, she took her future career very seriously.

If track was for Tab a means of relaxation, she soon learned that, for Kay, it was a vocation. Underneath the rather flippant exterior, lay a vicious competitor. Kay had made up her mind early to be an Olympian and pursued that goal with grim determination. After ten years, she wore the determination like a badge.

The road to the Olympics had not been smooth. Kay had dreamed of making the team as a middle-distance runner. It had taken Bill Bordeaux five years and an ulcer to convince her that her future lay in the marathon. He promised her that the women's marathon would be, one day, part of the Olympics and when his prediction came true he behaved as if he had accomplished the inclusion single-handedly.

It was a curious relationship, Tab thought, the union of an old-fashioned chauvinist—his great fault tempered by the fact that he was a true gentleman—and a strong, proud woman. Bill handled Kay like a fine racehorse—nervously and with respect. And Kay respected Bill and sometimes she felt sorry for him.

Caesar sank a claw into Kay's calf. Half-asleep, she swore and gave him a kick with her heel.

Tab picked up the cat and deposited him at the bottom of the bed. Then she turned out the light.

Chapter Three

Pop never threw anything out, Kay thought as she attempted to rearrange the boxes in the tiny cubicle that passed for the dispensary. If the piece of bread Alexander Fleming discovered penicillin in was still around, she suspected that Pop had it— somewhere in the miniature storeroom along with the twenty boxes of genuine horsehide trusses he had ordered in 1946.

At the moment, her problem was humidifiers. Pop had over-reacted during the flu season and ordered scores. Tomorrow, she would try to talk him into putting them on sale. "We can make it a two-for-one," she told Jean who operated the cash register. "They can have a humidifier for half-price, provided they agree to take a truss." She had piled the extra humidifiers in the dispensary and her immediate problem was finding a clear square foot of space in which to work.

She noticed the policewoman the minute she opened the door. It was cold outdoors on that April evening and she was wearing her winter greatcoat with the collar pulled up around her neck. Kay forgot about the humidifiers and made a pretence of checking the prescriptions that were stacked on top of the counter. The policewoman had purchased a chocolate bar and had paused to chat with Jean.

"Do you have my prescription?" a thin voice asked.

"Mr. Godkin?" Kay looked down quickly.

"The doctor said he was phoning it in."

"It's right here, Mr. Godkin." Kay checked one of the labelled packages. "You were due for a refill last week."

"Couldn't afford it last week. Did he order the generic?"

"Yes, he did." Kay glanced up again. Mr.Godkin was opening the package and examining the pills. The policewoman was still talking to Jean.

"They're the wrong colour."

"It's a new brand, Mr. Godkin." Kay took the pills and checked them anyway. "It's cheaper than the brand you were using."

"Oh."

"You've got to take these pills regularly, Mr. Godkin." Kay leaned across the counter. "You should be taking them exactly as the doctor ordered them. They don't work properly unless you've got the right amount in your system." She stapled the package and handed it back to Mr. Godkin. "When will you be eligible for your drug card?"

"Year and a half. I'm only sixty-three."

"OK." Kay straightened up with a smile. "Take the pills just the way it says on the label. Remember, three a day with meals —not two the way you were taking them before. OK?"

"Three pills a day, one with each meal."

"That's right."

Kay watched, shaking her head, as he walked away. Mr. Godkin couldn't afford the pills because he drank almost every cent he earned. Under those circumstances, she speculated, the pills probably weren't doing him any good anyway.

The policewoman had left the store. She was standing out front, waiting to cross the street. Kay waited until Mr. Godkin left then wandered down to the cash.

"Did you find room for the humidifiers?" Jean asked.

"Temporarily."

"If he'd leave the ordering to me, we'd be all right." Jean

shook her head. "Pop likes to have a hand in everything."

"I suppose after fifty years it's become a habit." The police-woman turned to the right and disappeared from view. "Has that cop been in here before, Jean?"

"No."

"Oh." Kay shrugged. "You seemed to be talking for quite a while. I thought maybe you knew her."

"She was just making friendly conversation. She's new down here. They've started up the foot patrols again."

"I thought they stopped foot patrols after that guy got his balls kicked in over on Gerrard."

"The police union demanded a moratorium on foot patrols," Jean said, quoting the newspaper. "The public demanded they be resumed. The union agreed as long as they got increased patrol car backup."

"It seems dangerous—a policewoman alone on foot. She's nothing but a target."

"She has radio contact with one of the cars all the time."

"Still it seems dangerous."

"I'm sure that she knows how to take care of herself. I suppose they get used to danger. It's part of the job. I'm glad she's down here. It makes me feel safer."

"I've always felt safe enough."

"So did I, until they held up that drug store last week. In the evening with everybody around. Just two blocks north of here. A bunch of kids looking for drugs."

"I guess I heard something about that."

"If they come in here, I'll be ready." Jean tapped the handle of her drawer confidently. "Raid. I'll let them have it right in the eyes."

"You won't do anything of the sort. They can strip the place clean for all I care. I'll gladly give them the drugs. I'll give them the equipment to shoot up. You can stand by and hand

20

them each a humidifier as they leave."

Jean was a serious, rather unimaginative woman but gradually she grasped the humour in the humidifiers. Jean found Kay rather unorthodox but, occasionally, she found Kay funny and, once in a while, Kay made her laugh. Tonight Kay made her laugh twice, once about the trusses and a second time about the humidifiers. This pleased Kay who imagined that Jean must, otherwise, have a boring life.

Kay went back to her cubicle and made coffee, then came down to the counter and Jean shared a sandwich with her.

While they ate, the policewoman passed by on the other side of the street.

Chapter Four

"It was a great dinner, Ma."

"I hope that it wasn't too far off your training diet."

"Roast beef with mounds of mashed potatoes and gravy is an integral part of my training diet."

"She means that she'll have to diet for three weeks now, Mom," said Tab who was loading the dishwasher.

"It's OK. Everybody has the right to get sloppy once in a while. Today, I feel like being sloppy." Kay went into the living room and settled herself comfortably with the newspaper.

Tab's mother followed with the coffee pot.

Kay said, "The apple pie, the apple pie was the best. "

"I'll give you the recipe."

Tab joined them in the living room. "Give the recipe to me, Mom," she said. "Kay can't boil water without creating a major catastrophe."

"I can cook." Kay removed the sports section. She gave the rest of the paper to Tab. "I don't have time to cook. That's the problem. I barely have time to eat."

"Peter," said Tab's mother, naming her favourite newsman, "says that eating has become too utilitarian. We spend an hour preparing a meal, rush through it in ten minutes and turn on the television. It's a shame."

"He's right," Kay murmured. "It's a shame."

"Do you want coffee, Kay?"

"Sure."

Tab's mother started to pour the coffee. "Oh, my," she said suddenly. "It's time for *Seeing Things*. Tab, turn on the television, please. Kay, you haven't said how you like my house."

A large white aspirin was break-dancing across the screen. "I love the house. It's too bad they had to put it in the middle of five square miles of strip development."

Tab had thought her mother would be offended. She wasn't. Kay had a way with her.

Tab's mother handed Kay the coffee. "It's not so bad. I know it doesn't look so nice right now but it will be a neighbourhood some day. I was talking to Mr. Luccini. He has a fruit market at the new mall. He says that he sees the same people more and more now. He's getting to know his customers. It's people who make a neighbourhood, Kay, not the way the stores are built."

"Every time I turn around out here there's a gas station or a God-awful shopping centre staring me in the face."

"People need gas stations and shopping centers. Otherwise, why would they be here?"

"The developers would love you."

The giant aspirin moon-walked off the screen.

"A CBC Special Presentation...." said the television announcer.

"What have they done with my Lou Ciccone!" Tab's mother gestured frantically. "Tab, hand me the TV Guide."

"A special look at the Canadian Olympic Team," the announcer intoned.

"You've been pre-empted, Mom." Tab stole a glance at Kay who was suppressing a guilty smile.

"If it isn't hockey, it's something else."

"Kay will be on the program, Mom."

"It was probably a rerun anyway."

23

"I think we're getting as bad at hyping our athletes as the Americans," said Tab with distaste.

The announcer was saying that Scott Wiggens had already set a new Commonwealth record. He had narrowly missed tying the world record.

"Yeah." Kay stretched lazily. She shook her head as the high jumper brought the pole down. "I think I like the way the Americans treat their athletes."

"They expect too much." Tab grimaced. "Imagine going to a track meet with the fate of the Free World riding on your shoulders."

Kay shrugged. "They think their athletes are the greatest. If they win, they're heros. If they lose, they still think they're the greatest. They just can't understand why they lost. We like to give our athletes the big buildup too. We make noises about how well we did at the Commonwealth Games, about how we're going for gold at the Olympics. Then, when we lose, they figure that we weren't so good after all. All of a sudden, everything we did before was a fluke. We love to make goats out of our heros."

"Pierre Burton would probably say that we don't believe that we deserve heros."

"Yeah," Kay laughed, "maybe we don't. Maybe winning is un-Canadian."

"Kay 'The Bishop' Strachan," the announcer said, "on her shoulders ride the hopes of our Olympic track team. *On the Road for Gold,* an in-depth look at Kay Strachan and her quest for Olympic gold. But first, this commercial message."

A group of juvenile males, let loose by their wives for the weekend, were extolling the virtues of a popular beer.

"I don't know if I like being sandwiched between a dancing aspirin and a bunch of paunchy fishermen."

"I rather liked the dancing aspirin," said Tab. "I thought it

24

was creative."

On the TV screen Kay was crossing the finishing line at the Boston Marathon. "Kay 'The Bishop' Strachan ," said the announcer. "She started walking at nine months, her mother tells us—even the nickname is prophetic—there is a stoicism, yes, even a monasticism, about the long-distance runner—"

"Do you think anyone will boycott the Olympics this year?" Tab's mother asked.

"I don't care," murmured Kay, intent on the screen, "just as long as the Aussies show up."

"You don't think that the Australians would boycott the Olympics?"

"Not unless our ambassador commits an unnatural act with a kangaroo."

"Kay!" Tab looked at Kay with a frown.

"It was just a joke, dear. Kay was making a joke."

"Mom, if I said something like that, you would be furious. Why does Kay get away with so much around you?"

"Because I'm not responsible for the way Kay turned out."

"Thanks," Kay said.

"Not that you didn't turn out well, dear." Tab's mother gave Kay a little pat on the arm. "Mothers are always harder on their daughters. Mine was."

"So was mine." Kay turned her attention back to the television screen.

Bill Bordeaux was saying that she was the greatest runner he had ever coached, a natural runner—a different kind of marathoner—refuses to be humbled by the distance—a killer without mercy....

"It's a good thing he said I was his greatest runner. Otherwise, I'd shoot him."

"Strachan is a loner," the announcer continued. "Perhaps all marathoners are loners—Strachan seems especially remote—her bonds with other Canadian Olympians, tenuous indeed—friends are mainly holdovers from the old days at the University of Toronto—there is an undercurrent that Strachan is not a team player—a rarity among modern Olympians—self-supporting—a bone fide amateur. Some say this is part of her peculiar snobbishness, an insistence upon being separate and different. A more charitable view is that it reflects the intensity of the woman, her single-mindedness, her refusal to be distracted or compromised. But, as one athlete put it: One thing you can be sure of is that Kay Strachan's gold medal won't be a victory for Canada or even for the Canadian Olympic Team. It will be a victory for Kay Strachan."

"I wonder which son of a bitch said that."

"Louise Patterson is our best chance in the fifteen hundred metres," the announcer went on. "She placed third in that event at the Commonwealth Games, finishing just seven seconds off the world record."

"Do you think that Louise has a chance, Kay?" Tab's mother asked. "Can she beat the American girl?"

"She'll be lucky if she finishes third or fourth in her heat. The Jamaicans won't beat the Americans or the East Germans or even the West Germans and the Jamaicans beat Louise. Seven seconds is like two hours."

Kay watched as Louise Patterson loped in slow motion across the screen. Louise, she thought, had beautiful form. She was terrific to watch. Unfortunately, she didn't have enough speed. She wasn't fast enough for the fifteen hundred and she wasn't strong enough for the three thousand.

Tab's mother said,"I heard someone on the radio compare her to Wilma Rudolph."

"That's because she's black." Kay shook her head in disbelief. "The jerks are comparing her to Wilma Rudolph because she's black and they don't have the brains to realize it."

26

"It must be hard when people think you don't have a chance," Tab's mother said sympathetically.

"She's the best we've got. She carries the flag well," Kay replied. "I mean, in the figurative sense. Some ugly weight lifter will carry the flag."

"My, that girl is sturdy." Tab's mother was referring to an East German runner who had just appeared on the screen. "Do you think she takes steroids?"

"I don't know. I've never heard that about her."

"I hear they have tests now. They can tell for months after."

"Well, if she shows up in Montreal looking like Miss Twiggy, we'll know for sure."

"They say some of the athletes do something called blood doping. They take their blood and save it and give it back to them before they compete."

"It's supposed to increase their oxygen-carrying capacity," Kay murmured. She was concentrating on the East German's quick choppy strides. The motion wasn't beautiful like Louise's but it was effective. "I didn't realize she was so short," she said suddenly.

"I beg your pardon?"

"Helga Weiner. I didn't realize she was so short."

* * *

"I hate that interview you gave after Boston," Tab said when they were in the car.

"I thought I was pretty good. I was close to being literate at times."

"You know what I mean. There was no need to say that you'd won the race for your boyfriend."

"I was referring to Bill." Kay shook her head as they merged with bumper-to-bumper traffic on the Allen Expressway. "Where in hell are all these people going? You know I was referring to Bill," she added.

27

"Sure." Tab switched lanes as she spoke. "I know it. Bill knows it. Perhaps a few intimates know it. What about the public? Does the public know you were referring to Bill?"

"I don't care what the public knows."

"As long as it doesn't know you're a lesbian."

"I don't care if the public knows I'm a lesbian. I just don't see the point of making an issue of it."

"Kay," said Tab, exasperated, "you're the most popular female athlete in Canada. You got twice as many votes in the last poll as little what's her name. You're a role model. If you were willing to speak out .... "

"I thought you were down on jocks this month."

"You're successful. You're high profile. You don't fit the stereotyped images. Young lesbian women need role models like you, Kay. When they hear the cheering, see the adulation, they need to know it's for one of them. They need to know that everyone knows it's for one of them."

"I don't want to be anybody's role mode. As an athlete—if they want me as a role model as an athlete—I suppose that's all right. I just don't want to be The Big Lesbian." Kay slid down in her seat with a yawn. "Let somebody else do it. Let Debbie do it."

"I don't think that Debbie's a good role model."

"Because she's a diesel-dyke?"

"She fits the stereotype. We don't need to reinforce negative images."

"Oh, ho!" Kay started to laugh. "You give me all this nonsense about physical appearance being unimportant, about how the emphasis on beauty degrades all women and now you're telling me that Debbie's unacceptable as a role model because she's a tough-looking broad."

"I didn't say that she was a tough-looking broad." Tab spoke rather uneasily.

"She makes Dave Semenko look like a wimp."

Tab ignored the remark. "A woman like Debbie reinforces the stereotype. She obscures the issue. Damn it, Kay, you know what I mean. Debbie is a big strong woman who thinks that being lesbian means imitating male behaviour. Debbie's no more representative of the lesbian woman than the whores in the men's magazines are representative of straight women."

"Such language!"

Tab gritted her teeth. "The point I'm trying to make is that the whores are not good role models and neither is Debbie."

Kay was amused. "What makes me such a good role model? A few days ago, I was macho slime. I was no better than Terry Kilroy."

"You're a successful woman. You have serious professional credentials. You have the capacity to raise public consciousness. It helps the cause if people are aware that their neighbourhood pharmacist—the helpful woman in the white coat—is a lesbian."

"It's because I'm good looking, isn't it?"

"God you're vain." Tab was changing lanes with abandon. "The fact that Gloria Steinem is attractive hasn't hurt the women's movement. In a perfect society, we wouldn't have to make compromises. The justice of the situation would speak for itself. In case you haven't noticed, we are not living in a perfect society. If we have attractive, personable women available, why shouldn't we take advantage of the situation?"

Kay rubbed her eyes wearily. "In other words, it's OK to be a whore as long as it's for a good cause."

"If you insist upon putting it that way."

"I don't want to be anybody's whore."

Kay expected a rejoinder but Tab wasn't speaking. As they passed under a street light, Kay could see that her face was set in that hard, determined expression—the one that meant that

29

she, Kay, had gone too far. The expression also meant that Kay had been correct enough in her assessments to make Tab angry.

Tab hated hypocrisy—especially in herself.

Chapter 5

Sunday was a rest day. Normally rest days felt good but, today, Kay felt tired.

She had run too hard the day before. Saturday was the long run—twenty-two miles along the dirt roads back of Kleinburg. Terry had been in a perverse mood and had paced her faster than the accepted practice pace. Every now and then, Terry couldn't resist reminding her that he could run faster than she could. His 2:14, while insignificant in the men's field, was still good enough to beat the fastest woman in the world.

Normally Kay ignored the challenge but, yesterday, Terry had been especially grating. Today, she tried to remind herself that Terry was unlikely to make the team and the juvenile excess was merely a cover for his bruised feelings.

Still, it was irritating that a man like Terry—even a sloppy, sporadically motivated one—might always run faster than a woman in top form.

She hadn't eaten properly over the weekend either. Tab had been out of the house most of the weekend. She had muttered something about food in the refrigerator but Kay hadn't felt like cooking and Tab had forgotten to buy oranges.

Pop was acting up too. He was beginning to regret giving her the three weeks off for the Olympics. With the week he had granted her for the National Capital, he reminded her, her leave amounted to an entire month. It was reassuring, Kay thought as she tapped some pills into a container, that Pop could still count.

God! She stopped and stared at the container, shaking her head. She had mixed up the prescriptions. She emptied the container quickly.

She had weighed in four pounds light after the run Saturday—and that was after fluid replacement. Bill wasn't going to like that. He was already miffed that she had agreed to open the shop for Pop on a Sunday. Sunday was his day, the day he reviewed her training schedule. More important, it was the day that Tab whipped up a gigantic brunch of bacon and eggs.

Kay glanced about the dilapidated dispensary with a sigh. It was just as well she had agreed to work. Tab probably wasn't at home anyway. As a consolation to Bill, she had invited him to lunch.

She didn't look up when the door opened. People came in all the time to browse. When Pop wasn't there, they would read the magazines and leave. Perhaps they took the magazines with them. She couldn't have cared less. The intruder moved up and down the narrow aisles, leather heels clicking against the hardwood floor. Kay picked up the control sheet and began to check the expiration dates on the dusty bottles behind her.

A bottle of digoxin wedged between two giant bottles of diuretics had disintegrated into a fine powder. The date on the label said: 1978. Kay set the bottle aside, baffled.

Suddenly she was aware that the clicking heels had stopped directly in front of the counter.

"Excuse me." The policewoman was looking up at her with a smile.

"Can I help you?" Kay removed her glasses, taking some time to tuck them into her pocket in an attempt to mask her surprise.

"I'm here to pick up a prescription. Brennan."

"OK." Kay began to check through the stack of prescriptions on the counter. "Brennan," she muttered. She paused, her face flushing suddenly. Birth control pills! "I'll have to go down to the cash to ring these in," she said. She tried to sound natural but her voice had taken on an edge.

The policewoman followed her to the cash. She gave Kay a twenty and Kay made change, conducting the operation with —what she hoped would be—suitable indifference.

Then she remembered her professional responsibility. "Do you have any questions?"

"I beg your pardon?"

"Do you know how to use the pills?"

The policewoman looked blank for a moment. Then she smiled. "They aren't for me," she said. "I'm picking them up for one of the women down at the station. I hope that's all right."

"Sure, sure." Kay hoped that she didn't sound too relieved. "Well," she said, picking up the package to check the label, "if Holly Brennan has any questions, ask her to give me a call."

"I'll do that."

The policewoman paused for a moment in the doorway. Then she was gone.

Kay watched until she disappeared from view, then returned to the dispensary. The kettle had boiled dry. Kay took it to the sink and refilled it, wincing as the water hissed against the hot metal. Simultaneously the kettle began to leak in a pathetic yellow dribble. Kay put the kettle down with a thump. God, Kay, she told herself, you really aren't thinking today.

* * *

"So, Terry tells me he had you racing yesterday."

"Damn men! Why do they have to tell each other every thing?"

Bill waved his fork apologetically. "The son of a bitch—if

33

you will pardon me, Kay, for saying that—the son of a bitch was bragging."

"I don't know how you guys do it. You go fishing with him, you go drinking with him and you don't even like each other."

"Men don't have to like each other to be friends." He shook a finger at her. "I don't want you to do anything like that again."

"I got carried away, Bill. I felt good."

"You're not eating well either—that little salad." He gesturing disparagingly at her plate. "That's not good enough."

"I'm not hungry today."

"You look as if you haven't been hungry for a while. I'd guess you've lost five pounds."

"It's only four, Bill."

"Four!" He shook his head. "I thought it was only two or three."

"Tab's been out. I don't eat well when I'm alone. You know I hate cooking for myself."

"Have Tab make some snacks for you then."

"She'd love that." Kay looked at her plate without enthusiasm. The salad seemed to wilt before her eyes.

"At least have a bagel." Bill pushed the bread basket toward her. "Ludden's training isn't going so well," he said. "She has a sore knee."

"I heard she was having trouble with her achilles."

"No, it's her knees. Too much running on the hills. The downhills. They say she's a great downhill runner but she hurts herself. I don't think she'll be a factor in Ottawa."

"Hm." Kay spread a thin layer of butter on the bagel. "Even without the knee problem, I never thought she'd be a factor in Ottawa. Kipkie is the tough one. It'll be between Kipkie and me."

"There is a rumour that Ludden won't run in Ottawa," Bill said rather sourly. "Her people think that, if they declare her

34

as injured, the Committee will exercise its prerogative to grant her the third spot on the team."

"Frost could be a problem if she decides to run away with it," Kay said. "If Frost has a great time—if anybody has a great time—the Committee will have a hard time justifying awarding the third spot to Ludden."

"Frost will go out fast but she'll die," Bill said confidently. "She doesn't have the endurance to be a front runner. She's inexperienced too. She doesn't know how to run a smart race. She can run a fast first half. She showed us that at Waterloo. It was a killer pace, I tell you. She was counting on the rest of the field going with her."

"The rest of the field did go with her."

"It was a Mickey Mouse race. I don't know where the coaching was."

"Not everyone is smart like you, Bill."

"Sure." He looked at her seriously. "I wonder what they said about the coaching after the way you ran your first Boston."

"They must have thought you were pretty stupid."

"Yeah, well," he said with a shrug, "I know Jock Peterson and he's not stupid. Now Frost is a stupid runner. That will change. Someday she'll be a good runner."

"But not as good as me."

"She doesn't have your natural talent. Talent is a great thing when you put it in a smart runner. You have the genes, Kay," he said, reverently. "You were born with the recipe. Your father was a marathoner."

"He never did much. There are fifty-year-old women running faster than he did."

"An athlete can be a failure only in his own time," he said patiently. "They were great runners then. Pure runners. They didn't have the equipment and all that. They didn't know the things we know now. The ones who were running then, they

35

were born to it. Now, people think you can take any piece of meat and turn it into a world-class runner. They think that science will do it. Hills. Intervals. The right shoes. They think we can engineer the athletes now. And, what do you get? Athletes with glass legs. The old guys, Kay, they ran in bad shoes and in their bare feet. They didn't have the injuries we see now."

"Runners train harder now."

Bill brushed the remark aside."You don't get injured, Kay. When I saw you the first time, I knew you had the right material. When I knew you were George Strachan's daughter, I was sure. All these problems some of the marathoners have— They weren't born to do the marathon. We're trying to cram square pegs into round holes.

"Some people admire that—overcoming adversity and all that."

"There used to be genetic selection," he said calmly. "The dinosaurs trampled the ones who couldn't run. The injured ones got eaten, the way you see the little sick animals get eaten in The National Geographic."

Kay closed her eyes attempting to block out the images. "Bill, you know I can't stand to hear about the little animals being eaten."

"To pick the great runners, you should study the genetic material," Bill continued, unperturbed.

"You should be coaching the East Germans."

"I'm just saying that we put a lot of energy into people who don't have the material."

"Some of them succeed. Some of them are champions."

"Sure, but it's not a pretty thing to watch. They're on the knife edge, you know. When they get a twinge, you hold your breath." Bill paused, setting his plate aside. "I didn't grow up wanting to be a runner, you know," he said reluctantly. "I wanted to be a hockey player, like Elmer Locke and all those other guys."

"But you weren't big enough and the other kids wouldn't let you play."

"I didn't have the quick eyes or the quick hands. I wasn't meant to be a hockey player. So, I ran. But I wasn't meant to be a runner either. I had a lot of pain. I wasn't like you, Kay."

"All runners have pain."

"Sure." Bill dropped a cube of sugar into his coffee and stirred it before continuing. "You, Kay, you have pain when you push yourself to what is beyond all human possibility. But for runners like me, the pain is every day. You are never free from it."

"It takes a lot of guts, Bill, to persist in spite of pain."

"Sure it does. But it's not natural." Bill touched his temple lightly as if the gesture would clarify his point. "You see a cheetah running on the plain. He is an animal and he runs. It is pure and simple. Nature has made him that way. It is his survival. He kills the zebra and he survives."

"Sometimes the zebras get away."

"For a few days, a few weeks, they get away. It's an illusion. They get away because the cheetah is smarter. He thinks, perhaps, that the calories consumed in the chase might not be compensated for by the kill. The ones who weren't made to run are always on the knife edge."

"Should I be taking notes, Bill? Is there something in this that you want me to know for Ottawa?"

"What?" He looked at her perplexed.

"I wondered if this was an allegory. You know, the zebras can't hope to beat the cheetah on ability. They have to depend on the cheetah to make mistakes, not to be hungry enough and so on."

"There is no allegory," he said simply. "I'm just saying that

37

nature gives talents to animals for their survival. A cheetah is meant to be fast. All its genes are built for that purpose."

"The zebras don't survive."

"They weren't meant to." He shrugged. "They were meant to be food."

Kay sat back and watched Bill while he drank his coffee. His bow tie bobbed up and down with each swallow. She had never seen him look anything but neat and perfect. She suspected that his mind was equally neat and perfect. Bill, she thought, was a simple man. Not stupid. Just simple. He didn't permit his mind to be cluttered with non- essentials. His cheetahs were, probably, just that—beautiful animals who attracted him because they were meant to run. And his zebras were zebras—slow and dull, destined to be nothing more than a food supply for the big cats. She was not a cheetah and Ludden was not a zebra. She was just a runner with bad knees.

But, bad knees or not, Ludden still had a chance to be an Olympian. Kay suspected that that must be an affront to Bill's senses. She was on the verge of asking him, but he seemed to read her thoughts and pushed the bread basket toward her.

"Eat."

* * *

Pop didn't show up until three. He didn't offer an apology and he didn't offer to pay her overtime. Kay didn't mention that she had closed the shop for lunch, reasoning that it didn't matter anyway. She suspected that, the minute she left, Pop would lock up and spend the remainder of the afternoon in the storeroom, doing cross-word puzzles.

* * *

Tab was at the kitchen table, marking papers when she got home. Her brow was furrowed as she squinted at the impossible handwriting.

38

Kay gave her a pat on the head. Tab merely grunted."Looks like chicken scratches," said Kay, leaning over her shoulder.

"No one bothers typing for the tutor." Tab pushed the papers aside with a sigh. "No one cares if the tutor goes blind."

Kay sat down at the table and poured a cup of tea. "So, how was it?"

"How was what?"

"Your weekend?" Kay took a sip of tea. It tasted strongly of Javex. Tab had been sterilizing the teapot again.

"It was fine."

"Did you sleep with her?"

"Yes."

"Was she good?" Caesar tried to jump up onto the table. Kay caught him cleanly with an elbow and he fell back to the floor with a disgruntled thump.

"I don't know if I care to tell you that."

"I'm asking as a concerned friend." Kay stole a glance at Caesar. He was sitting at her feet, looking hurt and bewildered. She felt a brief stab of remorse. "I want all of your experiences to be good," she said.

"She pleased me."

Kay started to laugh. "How very proper! Well, what was it like? Was it one long marathon session, or did you have to get out of bed periodically for the accoutrements? You know— vibrators, chocolate sauce."

Tab grimaced."I'd rather not talk about chocolate sauce."

"I know. It took you weeks to get it out of the sheets."

"Never again."

"So it wasn't such a great idea."

"I don't think that Esther believes in accessories," Tab said thoughtfully. Caesar was whining and clawing at her knee. She picked him up and put him on the table beside her. "Some of the women were discussing that topic at dinner last night."

"So, what do the women think?"

"They're really not in favour of accessories, especially personal vibrators. They particularly disapprove of personal vibrators," Tab continued seriously. "Esther believes that the vagina is virtually nonresponsive sexually. She feels that vaginal sex is a norm imposed by society to justify male/female invasive sex for purposes other than procreation."

"Christ!" Kay made a face at Caesar who had stretched out comfortably in the middle of the table. He looked almost smug. "Does that mean I spent five dollars on a vibrator for nothing?"

"Not everyone agreed."

"Thank God."

Tab ignored the remark. She reached for the stack of papers again, obviously unwilling to continue the conversation. Kay watched her quietly, sipping at her tea and remembering how tired she was.

Tab broke the silence a few minutes later. "I have a favour to ask of you."

"Yeah?"

"I promised the women that you would speak at our meeting Tuesday."

"You promised them I'd speak to them on Tuesday!" Kay looked at Tab, bewildered. "Just what in hell am I supposed to be talking to them about?"

"I told them that you would discuss the role of women in sports." Tab didn't look at Kay. She entered a grade in her notebook and tossed the paper into the pile to her right. She picked up another paper.

"Shit!"

"Louise has agreed to speak too. I thought you might feel better if you had company."

"If Louise is speaking, why do you need me?"

"Louise is discussing the role of the black woman in sports."

"Jesus Christ," said Kay, irritated. "What happened to that Jesus-freak who was supposed to be talking this week?"

"Ann James is not a Jesus-freak," Tab said calmly. "She was scheduled to speak about the prejudicial effect of language in the Old Testament. Her interest in the subject is purely intellectual. The Bible is a very oppressive piece of literature."

"You're going to be struck by lightening one of these days." Kay shook her head. "I don't want to speak to your group."

"Kay, I promised." Tab looked at Kay, her eyes mildly pleading. "Please. For me."

Kay looked at Tab for a long moment. The idea of saying no to her made Kay feel abysmal, especially since Tab looked so hopeful. Kay said lamely, "I have to work until nine."

"I told the women you would be late."

"Oh." Kay rubbed her eyes wearily. "OK," she said, emitting a deep sigh. "What the hell. I'll do it."

"Great." Tab returned to her work.

Kay poured another cup of tea. "The policewoman was in again today," she said.

"Really."

"She came in to pick up a prescription."

"Hm."

"For birth control pills."

"Cute."

"My jaw must have dropped five feet."

"I'm sorry."

"As it turned out, she was picking them up for someone else." Kay shook her head ruefully. "When she told me that, I must have lit up like the CN Tower."

"How do you know the prescription was for someone else?"

"I know. She told me. Why would she lie about something like that?"

"Perhaps she's one of those unmarried women who doesn't

41

want anyone to know that she has a sex life."

"I know they weren't for her." Kay paused for a long moment. "She said they were for someone down at the station. So," she continued, "I phoned."

"Kay!"

"Just being a conscientious professional. The woman—Mrs. Whatever—was grateful for my interest. I asked if she had any questions or problems. She thanked me profusely."

"Did she have any problems or questions?"

"No."

Tab put her paper aside and turned her full attention to Kay. "What are you going to do now?"

"I don't know." Kay paused, shrugging slightly. She hadn't thought that far ahead. "Nothing." She looked rather subdued. "Maybe I'll just sit on it until after the Olympics."

"Maybe she won't be available after the Olympics."

"Then she will have missed a great thing," Kay said flippantly."

"You're afraid she might want some of your time. You might miss a training run or be, otherwise, disastrously inconvenienced."

"Yeah, maybe." Kay stared at her now-empty teacup. Caesar's purr was hypnotic. She could barely keep her eyes open. "I think I'll have a nap." She stood up. "Do you want to have a nap with me?"

"No thanks. I have to finish these papers."

"Come and work in the living room." Kay lingered at the kitchen door. "I sleep better when I can see you."

Tab looked at Kay, shaking her head. "You're a real suck, Kay." Nevertheless, she gathered up her papers and followed Kay into the living room.

Kay lay down on the couch and pulled the afghan over her. Tab sat down in the armchair and returned to her work immediately.

"Bill thinks you should fix me some snacks if you're going to be away at meals." Kay's voice was muffled by the afghan.

"What does he think I am? Your nutritionist?"

"Yeah," Kay yawned, "I think he does." She stretched sleepily. "I've lost five pounds. He's annoyed."

"You've got to learn to look after yourself," Tab said, aggrieved. "What are you going to do while I'm in North Borneo?"

"I'll eat at your mother's."

"What will you do if I move out?"

"Move out?"

"I might find someone I want to live with," Tab said casually. "It could happen. What will you do if I find someone I want to live with and move out?"

"Who knows?" Kay mumbled. "Maybe I could move into a convent. I hear they feed you well in convents."

"I'm sure you would do well at a convent."

Kay didn't respond and, for a few moments, the only sound in the room was the scratch of Tab's pen against the paper.

"Do you think you might move in with Esther?" Kay asked finally.

"I don't know." Tab paused, pen poised thoughtfully. "I'd have to be very sure we were compatible. It takes time to be certain of that. I like to be careful about these things."

"You let me move in," Kay reminded. "You didn't worry about our compatibility."

"What could I do?" Tab was writing briskly again. Caesar paused in the doorway, glanced about the room, then went straight to Tab. He wrapped himself around her legs and started to purr. "You were a basket case when Bonnie left you. I was afraid that you might end up at 99 Queen Street."

"Shit!"

The mention of her ex-lover brought the conversation to an

43

abrupt halt. Kay turned over with an emphatic thump and lay facing the wall.

Tab started to say something then changed her mind. Caesar jumped into her lap and vaulted to the arm of the chair. He curled up beside her elbow with a contented yawn.

Chapter 6

They were whizzing past Maple Leaf Gardens before Kay spoke. "Why did you do this to me?" These were the first words Kay had said since they left the meeting, the first either woman had uttered for several blocks.

Tab checked the rear view mirror for patrol cars. "You needed to have your consciousness raised," she said stoutly.

"The hell I need my consciousness raised!" Kay stared straight ahead, her expression set. "Christ, Tab, I've been up since six a.m.. I busted a gut to get to your stupid meeting. I didn't do that to have those intellectual twits jump all over me."

"They weren't jumping all over you." Tab brought the car to an abrupt halt at a crosswalk. An elderly Portuguese woman, clothed in black, meandered across the street pulling a laundry cart, apparently oblivious to the screeching tires.

Tab shook her head. "They were asking hard questions. They were challenging you. The meetings are designed as learning sessions, Kay. The comments and questions are not meant to be taken personally. Everyone understands that."

"I thought they were personal enough."

"Louise was challenged in the same way. She took it in her stride. It's an intellectual process."

"All they did to Louise was call her an Oreo," Kay grumbled. "They didn't carry on about how she was sacrificing the lesbian-feminist movement for a shoe contract."

45

"The woman apologized when she found out that you don't have a shoe contract."

"Sure," Kay said sullenly. "At that point she decided that I was just born selfish."

Tab turned onto Church Street, letting the speedometer drop to an idle thirty.

"Kay," she said patiently, "the women were merely trying to point out that your great potential to advance the cause is not being utilized. They were saying that your single-minded devotion to your sport is a liability in that respect i.e. You don't allow yourself the time to get involved."

"Don't those twits realize that my single-minded devotion is what's put me in a position to do whatever it is they want?" Kay shook her head, exasperated. "Did you notice that, when I was ranked fifth nationally, no one was abusing me like this? Did you notice that, Tab? Eh?"

"I noticed it." Tab brought the car to a halt in front of the apartment building. She turned off the ignition and doused the lights before continuing. "I noticed that no one was abusing you when you were fifth-ranked. Although,"she added, "God knows when that was."

"Four years ago," Kay said, folding her arms. She made no move to get out of the car. "What really got me was when they took the vote to go on record as opposing competition in sports. What in hell does that mean? They didn't even ask me to leave the room during the vote." She cast a steely glance in Tab's direction. She shook her head . "No, that's not what really got to me. What really got to me was when you voted in favour of the damned motion."

"You knew I would. I've been very open about my ambivalence toward competition."

"Couldn't you have voted for me just the same? Just because I was your friend being torn apart by a pack of hyenas?"

46

"Louise voted for the motion."

"If I ran like Louise, I would have voted for the motion too."

Tab looked at Kay for a long moment. "Louise is a beautiful runner. Sports are about more than gold medals." She paused her hand on the door handle. "I don't plan to sit here all night. Are you coming in?"

Kay didn't respond. Tab guessed she was still fuming. She was unlocking the door to the apartment when she heard the door downstairs slam. Kay was on her way up the stairs. Tab entered the apartment, leaving the door ajar.

"Jesus!" Kay tripped over the mat as she closed the door. "Couldn't you at least turn a light on?"

"The kitchen light's on." Tab walked into the kitchen and went straight to the refrigerator. She took out a grapefruit, cut it into sections and put it on a plate.

"Christ," said Kay in disgust, "it isn't even Tuesday."

"It is Tuesday," Tab replied nonchalantly. She held the plate toward Kay. "Do you want some?"

"Sure." Kay took a section and followed Tab into the living room.

Tab picked up Caesar and flopped into the armchair. Kay turned on the television set. Neither woman spoke for several minutes.

"So," Kay ventured as the news dissolved into a commercial, "how was it?"

"How was what?"

"You know." Kay looked at her a trifle anxiously. "My speech, how was it?"

"It was OK."

"OK? Just OK?" She monitored Tab's expression for a moment. "It was great. It was great, wasn't it?"

"It was great."

"You're just saying that."

47

"No." Tab paused. "I mean it. It was great."

"So, why didn't you say so in the first place?" said Kay, finally convinced of Tab's sincerity.

"Because your bloated ego doesn't need further boosting. If your head were any larger, Kay, Environment Canada could use you as a weather balloon."

"Thanks." Kay stood up and turned off the television and went into the bathroom.

Tab listened to Kay commencing her nightly routine. Pieces of clothing plopped into the baskets one by one. One item missed the basket. Tab heard it hit the floor. She knew it would be right there, next time she went into the bathroom.

Kay reappeared in the doorway. "Are you coming to bed?"

"Why not?" Tab stretched wearily. There was a huge stack of papers in her briefcase but she didn't have the energy to deal with first-year essays.

Kay pushed the covers aside and got into bed. She didn't pull up the covers immediately.

Tab glanced at her out of the corner of her eye as she passed the door on her way to the bathroom.

Kay was admiring her abdominal muscles. "I guess we jocks aren't so stupid after all," Kay said as Tab paused in the doorway.

Tab stood framed in the doorway. "I've never accused you of being stupid. I have, on occasion, called you illiterate. Terry Kilroy is stupid. You're illiterate."

"Thanks." Kay's voice was without rancour and, for a moment, Tab felt touched. Perhaps, secretly, Kay felt oppressed by her jock image. Perhaps she was yearning to explore her intellectual side.

Tab was about to give voice to these thoughts when Kay began to flex her biceps.

Tab shook her head and passed by into the bathroom.

48

Chapter 7

The National Capital Marathon was held the third week in May. It rained and it was a cold rain. A group of novice runners huddled at the back of the pack, shivering in their sodden cotton sweats. Kay glanced at them without feeling as she made her way to the front of the line.

Everyone's favourite master, seventy-eight-year old Anna Joyce, stood cheerfully among the throngs, resplendent in a yellow Gore-Tex and gleaming chronometre. She called out to Kay that she was hoping to break her 4:30 PR, her Personal Record. Kay wished her luck and passed on.

As she took her place at the front of the line, she paused and looked back over the rest of the field. A number of the elite runners were complaining about the size of the field. They would complain, Kay guessed, about any field that numbered more than ten. The size of the field never bothered her. In the big races, it was occasionally a crush getting to the line but, once there, the great flood of runners presented no problem.

Kay glanced about at the other runners on the line. Frost was there, looking tense. She reminded Kay of a nervous thoroughbred being loaded into the starting gate. Kipkie stared at her shoes. She seemed lost in thought. She was a tall, rather fragile-looking woman but Kay knew that the fragility was deceptive. Kipkie was strong.

Ludden was not on the line. Ludden had finally ground her

knees into the ground. With Ludden out, Kay guessed that Kipkie was feeling supremely confident about making the Olympic team. The only concern remaining for Kipkie was whether she wanted to finish first or second in the National Capital.

Frost went out fast, just as Kay had predicted. Kay settled into the pace she had planned and Kipkie followed a few yards back.

At the five-mile mark, Kay picked out Bob Derek and ran with him. Bob, a big affable guy, was a comfortable 2:28 marathoner. Bob chatted and Kay pretended to listen. The fragments she absorbed told her that Bob was having trouble with his achilles. He was hoping for a 2:26 effort but he was taking it easy for the first half. He was anxious to see how his leg would respond. He hoped to pick up the pace at the half-way mark. He asked her if she was going for the win but Kay merely shrugged. She ran with him until just before the thirteen-mile mark. At that point, Bob turned to her with a grin and told her she would have to find someone else to pace her. He was leaving her. To her surprise, he dropped back. She didn't see him again until he crossed the finish line, twenty minutes off his PR and in pain.

With Bob gone, she became more aware of Kipkie. Kipkie, she guessed, was three or four yards behind her. She could barely hear the soft, effortless steps on the pavement.

At the eighteen-mile mark, Kay caught up to Frost. She ran beside the front runner for two miles then, at the twenty-mile mark, pulled away. Frost was labouring. She was breathing hard and her gait seemed unnatural. Kay glanced at her watch. She guessed that she would finish in 2:28.

Between the twentieth and twenty-second mile, she moved up on a pack of male runners. This, thought Kay with a smile, was the fun part of the race—moving effortlessly through the group, picking them off one by one. The men hated being

50

passed by a woman—even by a world-class woman. They resisted to the last. The chins dropped to the chests and the arms lifted to the armpits. But, one by one, they dropped back.

Now there was no one left but Kipkie. The men in the lead pack were long gone.

At the twenty-fourth mile, she could feel Kipkie's breath against her shoulder. It held there until the twenty-fifth mile. Then it was gone.

The rain had let up but the streets were covered with puddles. Kay became aware of Kipkie when she splashed through one a half-mile later, spraying the back of her leg. Then, suddenly, she was at Kay's shoulder. Kay turned her head to glance at the woman. Her features were calm and she was staring straight ahead.

With the finish line in sight, Kipkie started to sprint. Kay shrugged and let her go. She crossed the finish line in 2:28:10. Kay followed, fifteen seconds later.

Someone handed Kay a blanket as she crossed the line. She took a moment to shake hands with the winner. Kipkie didn't seem too excited about her victory. She knew, Kay guessed, that Kay could have out kicked her to the finish line if she had chosen to do so. The victory was, therefore, a hollow one. Kipkie must have wanted the win badly because she had sprinted. But it didn't mean that much and she must know it. Making the team was the object of the exercise.

The third woman to cross the finish line was Pasderka, another collegian. Kay found out later that Frost had dropped out. Pasderka's time was just under 2:31. Kay wondered if Ludden had watched the race and wondered what she was thinking.

"It was a good race, Kay." Bill squeezed through the melee near the finish line. "You ran it just as we planned. It was maybe fast by a minute or so but that's OK. I don't think that you were feeling any strain. You look good."

"It was like a training run."

"I was surprised Kipkie sprinted," Bill continued. His loquacity amused Kay who guessed that he had spent the evening in Hull.

"Did you spend the evening in Hull?"

"You know, Kay, that I stayed with Georges Gagnon."

"Are you really surprised that she sprinted?"

Bill shrugged. "Well, I guess not," he conceded. "I guess she wanted to win the National Capital. It was tough on her though. Her time was just a few seconds off her PR. She doesn't show the strain on her face so much, but she doesn't look so good now. I think she's vomiting."

"Thanks for telling me that, Bill."

"But you are as fresh as a daisy," he said cheerfully. "I knew you would be. I'll bet we could have sat this out. But, you can't take a chance I guess. You never know what they might do. I hear this kid, Pasderka, set a 2:28 pace for the last half. She was cautious at the start, I guess. She must have had it in her to do a better first half. I don't know if she knows yet that she may have a chance to make the team. 2:31's a PR for her. She did a 2:34 at the OUAA."

Kay interrupted. "Are you nervous or something?"

"Me? Nervous? Of course not. Why should I be nervous?"

"Because you're around all this good horseflesh and you can't help but think how much better it would do in your stable."

Bill looked a little sheepish, then he smiled. "Hey, why should I care? I've got the best in my stable."

"Come on," she said, putting an arm around him, I'll buy you a beer."

She had a beer and Bill had three or four. He seldom drank, except after a race. After the third beer he got nostalgic and talked about the old days, about his Boston. Then he got irritat-

52

ing and talked about her first Boston. At that point, Kay piled him into the car and headed back toward Toronto.

Bill fell asleep around Kingston and Kay drove on, thinking about Pasderka and about Kipkie. Pasderka, Kay guessed, would be elated. She had established a new PR and had, perhaps, won herself a spot on the Olympic team. Kipkie, by now, would realize that it had been a nothing day and a nothing victory. She had beaten Kay Strachan but she had vomited and Kay Strachan hadn't even been trying.

Chapter 8

Kay didn't see Louise Patterson until the third week after the National Capital Marathon. Louise was riding a very high wave. She had just set a new Canadian record at the Toronto Indoor Games and, as she told Kay, she hadn't even felt pushed. She felt that she had speed to spare and she expected to run a personal best in Montreal.

Kay had been taking it easy, recovering from the Ottawa race. In spite of the relatively slow pace, Bill had refused to consider curtailing the length of the recovery period. He had worked out a training schedule—a modification of her normal prerace schedule—which he promised would deliver her to the Montreal Olympics adequately prepared. Attempting to recover from one marathon and peak for another in less than three months was less than ideal but there was nothing else to be done.

Pasderka had been awarded the final spot on the Olympic team. The word on Ludden was that she would be out of action indefinitely with nothing to look forward to but surgery and a long period of rehabilitation. Kay should have felt sorry for Ludden but she didn't. Ludden had been careless. In order to please her sponsors, she had pushed her uneasy knee to the point of no return, competing in one money race after another. So Kay did not feel sorry for Ludden and she rather liked what she had seen of the young Pasderka.

For the first couple of weeks after the National Capital, Kay had felt tense and restless. But, today, she felt amiable and relaxed. The morning workout proved that she had fully recovered from the Ottawa race. After the interval session, she took a swim with Louise and worked out in the weight room.

Everything was going according to plan.

"I'll bet your Dad was pretty happy about your record," Kay said to Louise as they took a seat in the cafeteria. The cafeteria was crowded and noisy—bristling with young, incompetent-looking people—but Kay was in too good a mood to let the congestion bother her.

"Yeah, he was thrilled." Louise took a bite of the alfalfa sprout sandwich and chewed it thoughtfully before continuing. "I had to do well, Kay. Before the race, he sat me down and reminded me of all the sacrifices he had made to give me the opportunity to compete, of all the sugar cane he had hauled on his back so that I could go to school."

"Louise, your father is a dentist."

"I know. I doubt if he's ever seen a piece of sugar cane. I don't think that a member of his family has hauled sugar cane in generations. My grandfather had a charter business and his daddy was a fisherman, a good fisherman with a fancy boat. There was enough money floating around to send Dad to U of T for an education and he didn't have to work the dining hall to afford his Gucci loafers and designer jeans."

"Parents like to feel they've made sacrifices," Kay said with a grimace. "They need to feel that they've had something to do with your accomplishments. My Dad's a great guy. He has very little to say, but every fibre in his body screams sacrifice. You know the story. If he hadn't had a wife and kid to support he might have made it to Boston. Hell, if I had known I was going to be standing in the way of another Tom Longboat, I would have considered not being born." Kay paused, looking a trifle

55

guilty. "Bill says Dad has given me great genes. I should be grateful."

"Genes!" Louise started to laugh. "The first time Bill met my parents, I knew he was looking at the meat. Afterwards, he grilled me like crazy. He wanted to know all about their athletic backgrounds. I think he was shocked when I told him that Dad's greatest athletic accomplishment is walking from the house to the car in the morning."

"Bill's heavily into genes."

"Yeah." Louise settled into her tiger's milk with a sigh of satisfaction. "Well, he was really pleased about the way you ran in Ottawa. He was proud of the way you followed the game plan. He was so afraid that you might try to out kick Kipkie at the finish."

"I didn't need the National Capital."

"Some of the guys on television made a big deal about Kipkie's win. They were saying that she had run a smart race, letting you pace her, saving her speed for the end and so on. The only guy in the booth with a running background was John Price. I thought he was going to die, laughing."

"What did John say?"

"He said: 'You know this is just a donkey-trot for Kay.' The booth was so still, you could have heard a pin drop. What do a bunch of old hockey groupies know about track anyway?"

"I wish I had raced against Thomas in the last year," Kay said suddenly, naming the Aussie who was touted to be her major competition at the Games. "I haven't run against Thomas in almost two years. I know that she's improved since then. I've improved a lot more. But what can you tell unless you've competed head to head?"

"I guess that every road race is different."

"Sure. You can't compare the times at all. It's apples and oranges. I wish I'd gone head to head with her in the last year.

56

I'd like to see how she handles the surges."

"What does Bill think?"

"He thinks that the surges will wear her down eventually. He respects her though."

They chatted for a few minutes about Graf and Tenari, Kay's other major competitors. Then Louise switched the topic to Tab. "Jenny," said Louise, mentioning the name of a member of Tab's group, "says that Tab and Esther are involved in a major power struggle."

"Come again?"

Louise lowered her voice. "Esther has a strong need to be the dominant partner in every relationship. Tab claims that she carries that aspect of her personality to bed with her. She won't let go."

"Tab told Jenny that!"

"She told the whole group that. It provided the focus for last week's meeting. Unfortunately, I wasn't able to attend."

"Shit!" Kay looked at Louise, shocked. "They talk about what they do in bed at these meetings?"

"They state the situation in very nonprovocative terms," said Louise, putting the emphasis on the non. "The idea is to take an objective look at the mechanics of the relationship.It doesn't work that way of course. It's like reading one of those novels where the action fades out at the critical moments," she said, laughing. "You have to fill in the blanks with your own dirty imagination."

"Tab never said anything to me."

"That's because she knows you would laugh and make gross remarks. Esther and Tab are going through a working through process. Tab takes it very seriously."

"Tab takes everything seriously," Kay grumbled. "She needs to loosen up."

"I think Esther's the one who needs to loosen up. I suspect

57

Tab would try anything in bed—at least once."

"You're getting me excited, Louise. I'm in a recovery period. I'm supposed to be serene. But, you're right, Tab would try anything in bed at least once."

"I think that's great," Louise said seriously. "My last lover wouldn't let me touch her below the waist. Boy, was that frustrating! She was gorgeous too. It killed me."

"She was gorgeous below the waist?"

"She was gorgeous everywhere," Louise said with a sigh. "But," she added, "I don't think that Esther's need for dominance—in bed or out—is Tab's real problem."

"No?"

"No. I think she's upset because Esther's a better cook."

"You've got to be kidding."

Louise shook her head. "Did you know that she's signed up for gourmet cooking classes?"

"She didn't tell me that," said Kay, a trifle annoyed. "Does this mean I'm going to get watercress sandwiches with the crusts trimmed?"

Louise wagged an accusing finger at Kay. "There! You see! You don't take her seriously so she's decided not to tell you anything anymore. She's guarding. She's head over heels in love with Esther. They're having a few problems and she doesn't want any jokes from you about it."

"Head over heels, eh?" Kay was quiet for a moment.

Louise finished her tiger's milk, casting an anxious eye in her direction. Kay was staring moodily at the tablecloth. "Look, Kay," she said, setting the glass aside, "I hope I didn't say anything to upset you."

Kay shrugged. "You didn't upset me."

"You look awfully thoughtful."

Kay fixed Louise with a long, level gaze. Then she laughed. "I was just trying to decide what to wear to the wedding."

Chapter 9

"Are you sure you won't have a sandwich?"

"I tell you, Jean, I am dying. I can barely handle my own saliva."

It was early evening at Pop's. Two of the overhead lights were out and Jean's round face hung like a full moon in the glow of the gooseneck lamp. "I've never been to a dental hygienist," Jean said sympathetically. "I thought all they did was clean your teeth."

"I had plaque down to my toes." Kay leaned over the counter, grimacing at the memory. "She spent two hours, scraping plaque off my roots."

"Plaque?"

"Yeah. It's what you get when you don't floss. God gets mad when you don't floss. He gives you plaque."

Jean wasn't sure whether Kay was kidding or not. "Did you have any cavities?"

"Yeah, one tiny one no bigger than a pinhead. The dentist filled it without freezing. After the dental hygienist, the filling was a treat."

"I've never had plaque," said Jean, fascinated by the word.

"That's because you've never been to a dental hygienist."

The phone rang. Kay picked it up, spoke briefly and handed the receiver to Jean. Then she shifted her attention to the prescriptions in front of her.

"It's my kid," Jean said when she hung up. "He wants me to meet him at the subway stop. He's going to a movie at the Eaton's Center and he forgot his money. Can you mind the cash for a minute, Kay?"

"Sure thing." Kay tapped out a label for the prescription, put the bottle of pills into the bag and set the bag aside.

"Should I get some ice cream for you while I'm out?"

"Please don't. My gums throb at the very thought."

"I'll bring you a milk shake. I'll ask the girl to warm the milk."

Jean was out the door before Kay had a chance to object. Kay opened the door to her cubicle and walked slowly down to the cash. Jean, she thought as she slid onto the stool behind the cash, could never disguise the fact she was a mother. She would come back with a milk shake and a bowl of soup, for good measure. And she, Kay, would have to eat it. Otherwise Jean's feelings would be hurt. Kay opened the newspaper and started to read.

The door opened and closed softly. Kay could hear the customer moving quietly along the middle aisle. She didn't bother looking up. If she was going to be robbed, she told herself, she didn't want to know about it in advance.

She didn't see the policewoman until she stopped in front of the counter. She had a smile on her face and a package of Band-Aids in her hand. "Hi."

"Hi." Kay removed her glasses with deliberate sensuality and tucked them into the pocket of her lab coat. So pleased was she with the smoothness of the act that it took her a few moments to realize that the cop's left hand was bleeding. She had wrapped it in a tissue but the blood had seeped through in a round, fresh stain.

"I stopped to help a motorist change a tire," the policewoman explained, noticing Kay's gaze. "I caught my finger in the jack. It was stupid."

"Looks like you did a pretty good job of it," Kay said.

The policewoman didn't move. She stood in front of the counter rather helplessly, as if she couldn't decide whether to bandage her finger first or pay for the Band-Aids. She had already opened the package and was holding a Band-Aid in her hand.

"Would you like me to clean the cut?"

"That would be great."

The smile was terrific, the curve of the lips beautifully disconcerting. Finally Kay realized that she had been staring for an awkwardly long time. She led the cop quickly to the dispensary.

The stainless steel sink was tiny. That, together with the clutter created by Pop's excess stock, dictated that they stand at the sink virtually shoulder to shoulder. The tissue slipped off to reveal a rather angry-looking cut.

Kay washed it carefully with soap and water. "Do you have to report this down at the station? Fill out forms and so on?"

"I can't be bothered. If anyone notices, I'll say I cut my finger peeling potatoes."

"Well," said Kay, reaching for a bottle of alcohol, "I'd better put some of this on it. It'd be a bugger if your finger fell off and you hadn't filled out the WCB forms."

The word bugger slipped out without warning. The policewoman, apparently not offended, laughed. "I guess I'm lucky I didn't get a lot of grease in it."

"Sure." Kay clamped the Band-Aid in place with more authority than she had intended. "I'd hate to see you end up with lockjaw."

The policewoman flexed her finger to test the repair job. "Thanks. That's great."

Kay thought it was the sloppiest bandage she had ever seen.

61

It looked totally out of place with the crisp, neat uniform.

"Well, at Pop's we aim to please," she said. "That is, as long as Pop isn't here. If Pop was here, he'd charge you a rental fee for the sink." Kay made the remark then chastised herself almost immediately for her flippancy. A nice you're welcome would have sufficed.

The cop followed Kay back down to the cash. She stood, wallet poised, while Kay tried to master the vagaries of the cash register. First, she made an incorrect entry. Then the paper jammed. Finally the stubborn machine cooperated and she handed the policewoman her change.

"Thanks." The policewoman put the change into her wallet then dropped the wallet into her jacket pocket. "Have you ever been to The Mayflower," she asked suddenly.

The name of the lesbian bar caught Kay off guard. She jerked her head up in surprise.

"No," she said quickly, "no, I've never been there."

"Oh," the policewoman said, staring at the floor, "I'm sorry. I thought I'd seen you there."

Kay attempted a smile."Well," she said, "I guess a lot of people look like me." She was about to add that, according to Bill, she looked like half the Indians on the St. Regis reserve but changed her mind.

"I guess so. It's a big city." The policewoman smiled but she still looked disappointed. "Well," she said, indicating her finger, "thanks again for the repair job."

"You're welcome." Kay watched until the policewoman disappeared from sight. She felt inordinately depressed.

Jean returned within minutes. She had a chocolate milk shake and a Styrofoam bowl full of lukewarm mushroom soup. The soup had little aesthetic appeal but it was filling and Jean's company was comforting. Together, they dispelled the gloom temporarily.

* * *

Kay was surprised to find Tab at home when she returned from work that evening. She was even more surprised to find Tab alone. "I've had a rotten day."

Tab was at the kitchen table, toiling over a stack of papers. She addressed Kay without looking up. "You sound a little depressed."

Kay flopped into the chair opposite Tab. "I struck out twice and my mouth feels as if a herd of centipedes is doing a tap dance across my gums."

"Do you want a brownie?"

Kay hesitated, then took one from the plate Tab pushed forward. "This is the first solid food I've had all day." She motioned toward the papers. "Are you still marking those things?"

"This is a different set." Tab's hair was tousled from being twisted between her thumb and forefinger. "This is the take-home exam for Sociology 080. It's a crock, of course. The kids obviously collaborated on the answers. They've rearranged the sentences a bit to fool me. One group has used inverted sentences and so forth."

"I spent an hour today, lying in a reclining chair with my head against the breast of a gorgeous woman," Kay said, shaking her head regretfully. "and I couldn't even enjoy it. I was in agony."

Tab said patiently, "I've told you a hundred times that you should have your teeth cleaned at least once a year. What do you expect when you have five years of accumulated plaque?"

"I don't want to hear the word plaque again," Kay said testily. "I'm going to kill Bill when I see him. Suddenly, out of the clear blue sky, he gets the idea that I should have my teeth cleaned. 'We don't want you developing a toothache in Montreal,' he says."

"Bill's right."

63

"Yeah, well." Kay started to argue the point, then decided she was too tired. She sat back, munching her brownie and watched Tab work. Caesar entered the room, crossed the floor and worked his way languidly around her legs. She threw him a crumb. He examined it without interest and wandered off to his food bowl. He sat there for a moment, hopefully, then stretched out and began to wash his paws.

"The policewoman was in again," Kay ventured finally. "It was the perfect setup. Jean had to go out on an errand. There wasn't a single other customer in the store. I even got to patch up her finger."

She described the event to Tab in detail. "Then," she said with a sigh, "we were at the cash and she was asking me if I'd ever been at the Mayflower. For some reason, I froze. I acted as if I'd never heard of the Mayflower."

"Did you think she was asking for the wrong reason?" Tab didn't look up from her work but the tone in her voice indicated renewed interest.

"No," Kay said, shaking her head, "I thought she was asking for the right reasons. She's interested."

"What is the problem then?" Tab put the papers aside and turned in her chair to face Kay. "I would have thought that you would like that."

"I almost said yes," Kay said thoughtfully. "Then, in five seconds, it all flashed in front of me. Christ, Tab, if I had said yes to the Mayflower the next step would have been coffee after work. We'd have to talk. I don't think I have the energy for that. Hell, everything in my life is so focussed right now. Every little extra thing seems like a huge burden. I'm glad I'm going to Montreal a week early. I need to get away from all this— from Pop's and from all the rest of it."

"Am I a distraction? Perhaps I should move out."

"No." Kay stared at the sugar bowl moodily. "You eliminate

the distractions—like looking for food, finding clean under-wear."

"I'm glad you noticed," Tab said dryly. "I was beginning to wonder if you thought we had a hired maid." She looked at Kay for a moment, then said with a shrug, "Why don't you invite the woman for coffee? Explain that you want to get to know her better. Explain that, once you get your gold medal, you might actually become human again and be prepared to do a few fun things."

"I think I'll tell her that after I get the medal."

"Tell her now." Tab's voice had an imperative ring to it.

"What's the rush?"

Tab looked at Kay wearily. "Don't you realize that this is the first woman you've mentioned more than once in the past three years? That must mean something. If I wasn't so con-venient, you'd be a nun."

Kay was suddenly subdued. "I like her, but I think it can wait for another month."

"You thought Bonnie could wait for another month too."

"I didn't leave Bonnie," Kay said defensively.

"Leave her!" said Tab, a trifle incredulous. "You literally ran away from her. Your head was somewhere else—the Bos-ton Marathon, the Chicago Marathon, the Osaka Marathon. She changed majors. You didn't notice. She came very close to a mental breakdown. You didn't notice. You were so wrapped up in yourself that Bonnie could have died her hair purple and you wouldn't have noticed."

"I didn't walk out on her." Kay paused, swallowing hard. "I was working my guts out and she ran off on me with that bank teller—that fat, bitch of a bank teller."

"That's what really bothers you, isn't it?" said Tab, ignoring Kay's expression. "She had the nerve to run off with a fat wom-an! She had your great body at her disposal and she chose to give it up for a fat woman!" Tab paused, shaking her head. "A lot can happen in a month."

Kay was quiet for a moment then, unexpectedly, she started to laugh. "I almost forgot," she said triumphantly. "You're going to North Borneo in September. You want to get me squared away before you leave. You're so organized."

"I don't want you to get depressed." Tab's voice was full of concern. "I know how you hate being alone. You were pathetic when Bonnie left."

"Maybe I got tougher after that." Kay stood up. She touched Tab's hair and started toward the bathroom. "Do you want to have a shower with me?"

"No thanks." Tab was once again absorbed in her papers. "I had one this afternoon," she added.

"When did you have a shower?" Kay appeared in the doorway, pulling her shirt over her head. "I was here most of the afternoon."

"I didn't say that I had the shower here."

"Oh." Kay surveyed Tab, nodding her head in amusement. "Love in the afternoon. Being a tutor must be great."

"It has its advantages," Tab said calmly.

Kay turned back into the bathroom, laughing. Tab could hear her laughing even as she stepped into the shower and turned on the water. For a few moments, there was no sound other than the thunder of the running water. Then Kay began to whistle.

Caesar flicked an ear in irritation and stalked angrily from the room. Tab shook her head.

Chapter 10

The policewoman didn't come back to Pop's that week but, when Kay arrived for work the following Monday, she saw her standing on the opposite corner talking to two policemen in a patrol car. A small crowd milled about the intersection, watching as a tow truck hooked a cable to a battered automobile. When Kay went inside she found Jean pressed against the window, taking in the scene.

"What happened?" Kay asked the question more for the purpose of getting Jean's attention than from curiosity.

"Accident," said Jean still glued to the window.

"I sort of figured that." Kay leaned across the counter. "All that broken glass."

"Some guy came barrelling through a yellow light." For the first time, Kay realized that Jean was dazed. "Knocked Lily right into the lamp post. They just took her away in an ambulance."

"Lily who?"

"The baglady." Jean finally turned away from the window. "The one who hangs around the submarine shop."

"The one who wears the fur coat winter and summer?"

"That's the one," Jean said hoarsely.

"So," Kay said, fishing for something appropriate to say, "was she hurt badly?"

"I don't know," said Jean, shaking her head. "When I saw

67

her, she was lying against the lamp post. Guy," she said, naming one of Pop's regulars, "Guy was just in. He says she stepped into the intersection just as the light was changing. He says there was blood all over the place."

"I think I've heard enough." Kay turned toward the dispensary. She was hanging up her jacket when she realized that she was being insensitive. She walked back down to the counter. "Are you all right, Jean?"

"I'm OK," said Jean, subdued. "It's just that I've seen Lily every day for years. When you see someone every day you feel as if you know them."

"I know how it is," Kay murmured. Actually she didn't and she didn't have time to test her imagination. Pop had left a stack of prescriptions to be filled.

* * *

The policewoman came in Pop's at ten minutes to nine. Her shoulders were hunched and her cap was pulled low over her eyes. She didn't buy anything but stood for a few minutes at the cash, talking to Jean. Kay caught only snatches of the conversation but enough to surmise that they were discussing the accident. She waited until the policewoman was gone, then left the dispensary and walked down to the cash.

"She's dead," Jean said before Kay could ask any questions.

"I'm sorry," Kay said lamely.

"She's dead," Jean repeated. "The policewoman just got the word from St. Mike's. Massive internal injuries, they said."

"That's too bad."

"The policewoman's pretty upset." Jean leaned across the counter, her expression solemn. "She was the first one at the scene. I guess she knew Lily quite well."

"Yeah." Kay let her eyes drift toward the window. She could not see the policewoman.

"She just came in to talk. I guess she had to help clean up

afterwards."

"Jean, can you lock up?" Kay asked suddenly. "I promised someone I'd meet them at nine."

"Sure, Kay."

She caught up to the policewoman three blocks away. She was walking slowly, staring at the pavement. Kay fell into step with her. "Hi."

The policewoman looked up, startled. Her eyes were red-rimmed and a little puffy. "Hi."

"Do you remember saying that you thought you'd seen me at the Mayflower?" Kay said, stuffing her hands into her pockets. "Well," she said with a shrug, "I've been there. I don't know what I was thinking about when you asked."

The policewoman attempted a smile. "I guess all the bars look alike after a while."

"Yeah."

The policewoman did not respond. The silence made Kay nervous. "Look," she ventured, "if you're off duty, maybe we could go for a coffee."

"I'm not off duty until midnight," the policewoman said. There was a terrible pause, then she added, "But I'm on my break now." She smiled. This time the smile seemed a little brighter.

"Good. Is this OK then?" Kay indicated a coffee shop a few steps ahead.

"It's fine."

Kay pushed open the door and they went inside. It wasn't until they were seated that she realized they hadn't exchanged names. "Hey," she said, trying hard to sound casual, "it just occurred to me that I don't know your name."

"Mary Johnson," the policewoman said, offering her hand.

"Mary Johnson," murmured Kay. She shook the police-woman's hand, feeling slightly rattled. "Hey, it should be Mary

O'Brien. You've got red hair. You should be Irish and your name should be O'Brien."

She stopped, suddenly conscious of the fact that she was still holding Mary Johnson's hand. "Oh." She released her grip, "my name's Kay, Kay Strachan."

"I know," Mary smiled. "I've watched you train. I've seen you on television too. I watched you in the National Capital."

"That was a shit race." The word came out without warning and Kay blushed. Mary didn't seem to be perturbed. "I mean, I didn't win," Kay explained. "I'm a lot better in the races I win."

"The papers said you ran a good race. They said you were smart not to try to out kick Kipkie at the end."

"Yeah, it was smart. I don't have the greatest kick around but I could have out kicked her."

The waitress pulled to an abrupt halt beside the table.

"Coffee," Kay told the waitress. She looked at Mary."Do you want anything else?"

"I don't think so."

"Are you sure? I'll bet you use up a lot of calories,walking the beat."

"No thanks. I'm not very hungry tonight."

"Two coffees."

The waitress left and Kay thought that Mary looked sad again. "Jean told me what happened," she said rather abruptly, "I'm sorry."

Mary didn't respond for a few moments and Kay was afraid that she was going to cry again. "I always wanted to be a cop," Mary said finally. "My Dad's in the Ontario Provincial Police, the OPP. He talked me out of that. He said that twenty-five years of scraping bodies off highway 400 was twenty-five years too many. He persuaded me to join the Metroforce instead. He thought that being a city cop would be cleaner."

70

"I wouldn't want to be a cop of any kind."

"I've been on the force for six years," Mary continued. "I've seen some pretty rotten things. But tonight—well—tonight got to me."

The waitress brought the coffee and Mary fell silent.

Kay said, "I guess accidents are pretty messy."

Mary stared at the tablecloth. "It wasn't that. I have seen messier things. At first I thought it was all right. She was still conscious when they put her in the ambulance. She was talking to me. She couldn't find her purse and she was worried that someone had stolen it. I found the purse when the tow truck came to haul the car away. It was snagged in the under-carriage."

"Some of the bagladies have a lot of money tucked away."

"There wasn't any money." Mary continued to stare at the table. "Just a few cents. There was some food—an apple with a bite out of it, a dried-up sandwich. Everything in the purse was junk."

She paused, wiping at the corner of her eye with her sleeve. The words came haltingly. "There was an old pocket watch with one hand missing, an old wallet with nothing in it. There was a dog collar with a tag." She stopped, swallowing hard. "Jesus, that's what got to me. I was tagging the stuff with the Sergeant when they called to say that she was dead. The Sarge was holding the dog collar. He looked at it and looked at me. That's what got me going." She raised her eyes to look at Kay. "The woman was dying and all she could think about was her purse."

Kay met the gaze solemnly. "Yeah, I guess that's all she had. So," Kay said with an awkward laugh, "why do you want to be in this business anyway? There's got to be an easier way to earn a living."

"I've never considered doing anything else." Mary paused to

71

sip at her coffee. "I like my job. When something like this happens, it is hard to take. But," she said with a sigh, "maybe it's things like this that remind you that you're human. Maybe they make up for the times you should have felt badly and didn't. You know what I mean. You must see sad things in your work too sometimes."

"Sure." Kay felt a stab of guilt. She tried to think of an appropriate anecdote but nothing came to mind. She had never allowed herself to dwell upon the little human tragedies that faced her everyday at Pop's. She didn't want to tell Mary that she never thought of the people and that Pop's was just a way station enroute to a gold medal. "At least people trust pharmacists," she said finally. "People don't trust cops. Don't you find that tough? Knocking your brains out to help people when half of them think you're the enemy?"

"In a big city a lot of people are the enemy if you don't know them. That's what's so important about the foot patrols. People get a chance to know you. I didn't know how well I was doing until today. A lot of people wanted to help—the kids from the submarine shop, the old lady from the newsstand. All of a sudden, I felt as if I was one of them, a part of the neighbourhood."

Mary paused, searching Kay's eyes hopefully for a note of recognition. "You must feel as if you're one of them. You run the same route every day. You see the same people.They've seen you on television, read about you in the newspapers. You must be part of the landscape to a lot of people down here."

Kay felt like saying that it was a jungle out there, a jungle full of obscene creatures who fed off what they imagined to be the fear they created in those they considered weaker. Full of scum who couldn't stand the sight of a male runner, much less a female runner. "Yeah," she lied, "I feel real close to the city." She couldn't bear to disturb Mary Johnson's new-found sense of community.

"I know that some runners have trouble," Mary confided, "but it must be different for an elite runner."

"Sure," Kay said flippantly, "people tend to pelt you with a higher grade of garbage."

"You're kidding! People throw garbage at you!"

Kay shrugged, then broke into a smile. "Yes,I'm kidding. I'm too fast to get hit with garbage anyway."

She was debating whether or not to tell Mary about the beer can that had narrowly missed her while she was running near Kleinburg when a loud crackling noise intervened.

Mary reached for the walkie-talkie that hung in her belt and held it to her ear.

"Trouble?" Kay asked as Mary put the transmitter away.

Mary smiled and shook her head. "Nothing serious. Just a bunch of kids hanging around in front of Warner's Variety. The manager phones in a complaint almost every night. The kids camp out front just to bug him. He feels they're a deterrent to his clientele."

"Knowing the kind of clientele you get around here, you'd think he'd appreciate a deterrent," Kay said. "No,"she added as Mary reached for the bill, "I'll get it."

Mary said,"Thank you," then picked up her cap. She settled it on her head with an elegant flourish.

Kay guessed that she had learned the manoeuvre by watching her father and that it was now a matter of habit. She decided to accompany Mary to Warner's Variety although it was several blocks out of her way.

The kids were sitting on the front steps, smoking. A ghettoblaster rested on the sidewalk in front of them. Even turned to full volume, the machine was no match for the stream of loud, course language.

"Looks like trouble to me," Kay said.

Mary just smiled. "They're pussycats. They want a little attention. They'll move on when I ask them to. It'll take a few minutes, of course. They'll want to negotiate. They don't want it to look as if they were run off by a woman but they'll go."

"Are you sure?"

"Yes." Mary looked confident. "They know, if there's any real trouble, a patrol car will show up. They don't want to risk that. They want to talk to someone who will treat them nicely. They don't get much of that—not even at home."

"I suppose you're going to tell me that you're their mother figure."

"Sort of. Maybe a sister figure."

"Don't you think you should call for backup?" Kay suggested nervously. "There are six of them."

"No. Sometimes male cops bring out the violence in these kids." They were close to the group and Mary lowered her voice. "I should say good night right about here."

Kay eyed the group suspiciously.

"I'll stop by Pop's tomorrow."

"OK." Kay murmured good night and passed the group quickly, eyes averted.

"New girlfriend, Mary?" one of the kids called out.

"Just giving directions to an out-of-towner," Mary said calmly.

Kay crossed the street at the next light. She considered going back toward Pop's but changed her mind. It was the most direct route home but she was aware that she was still under surveillance. She continued up the street away from Warner's, glancing back once. The kids had turned the radio off and were hovering about Mary, listening intently. Mary stood at the center of the group, talking quietly. She seemed totally in control.

Kay turned and hurried on.

* * *

When she got home, the apartment was dark. The sound of

74

her key in the door brought Caesar from his perch on the kitchen table. He wrapped himself around Kay's legs as she groped for the light switch.

There was a note on the refrigerator:

I don't know what time I'll get home. Please feed Caesar. Give him one-quarter of a cup of canned food and one-half cup of kibble. Don't forget to add a teaspoon of vegetable oil. Thanks—Tab
P.S. I threw out three pairs of your underwear this morning. They weren't worth repairing. Buy more!
P.S. Make sure that Caesar's food is at room temperature. If it isn't, he'll vomit.

Kay put the note aside with a groan and opened the refrigerator door. There was half a melon wrapped in plastic on the second shelf. She took it out along with a quart of skimmed milk.

Caesar cried piteously as the refrigerator door closed. Kay opened the door again and took out the cat food. The can was half-full and sealed neatly with a plastic lid. The food was ice-cold.

Kay set the cat food on the counter and sat down at the kitchen table with the melon. Caesar vaulted to the table and nosed the milk carton hungrily.

"You know you can't have that," said Kay, rescuing the milk. "Milk gives you diarrhea. You're going to have to wait until your food warms up. I'm not going to have you barfing on the rug."

God, she thought, I'm talking to the damned cat!

She made Caesar wait for half an hour. By that time, he

was petulant and merely nosed at his food.

Tab did not come home that night. Caesar vomited a little on one corner of the rug to show his general displeasure.

Chapter 11

Thursday was an interval day. Kay worked out on the track with Louise under the watchful eye of Bill Bordeaux. Terry Kilroy appeared halfway through the session for nuisance value.

Kay was pleased with the workout but Louise seemed depressed. "My hamstrings feel tight," she told Kay afterwards in the whirlpool.

"Yeah?" Kay was enjoying the water and contemplating how nice it was to be rid of Terry Kilroy—albeit temporarily. Terry had invited himself to join them for an afternoon snack.

"I was afraid to go all out today," Louise continued. "I could almost hear the muscles ripping. " She stared into the bubbling water, her deep brown eyes almost morose. "I could imagine everything tearing off the tendon sheaths, everything letting go, the tendons withering and shrivelling.... "

"Sounds like a Grade B horror flick," Kay interrupted. She let her hand drift delicately over her own hamstring. She felt nothing but pleasant fatigue.

"When the hamstrings tear, you can fall flat on your face. In a race, someone can run right up your back." Louise looked at Kay beseechingly. "Do you ever worry about falling in a race and being trampled by the pack?"

"No."

"What do you worry about?"

"I don't worry about anything."

"Side stitches? Dehydration? You've got to worry about

something."

"No." Kay shook her head. She was silent for a moment. "OK," she acknowledged at last, "when I first started to run the marathon, I used to worry about not finishing, about pacing myself incorrectly and not finishing, about hitting the wall and not finishing, about getting a side stitch and not finishing. Now I feel as if I have control over all that. I don't worry anymore. What is it Mickey Rivers used to say? Something like: 'If you've got control over things, there's no sense worrying about them because you've got control. If you haven't got control over things, there's no sense in worrying because you can't do anything about it anyway.'"

Louise looked at Kay with a pained expression.

"It makes perfect sense. Mickey Rivers always makes perfect sense."

"Who in hell is Mickey Rivers? "

"A baseball player. A black baseball player."

"I don't know a thing about baseball", said Louise. "My Father's heavily into cricket though. A gentleman's game."

" Yes, sticky wicket and all that."

Louise let her head flop back against the edge of the tank and stared at the ceiling reflectively. "When I was in high school, I fell during a race. I've never been sure if I pulled my hamstring and fell or pulled the hamstring when I fell. I was boxed in with another runner right on my heels. I think she stepped on the back of my shoe and I started to tighten up. It was like being in the middle of a traffic jam on the 400. Then." She shook her head, "I fell. There was a horrible tearing pain in the back of my leg." Louise stretched her arms, cupping her hands behind her head. "Then she ran right over on top of me. That wasn't the worst part though."

There was a long pause. "There was a split second before it happened when I knew it was going to happen. I knew that she was going to run right up my back in those spikes. I could imagine her pushing off my neck, crushing the vertebrae, tearing my spinal cord to shreds. I lay on the track afterwards, waiting for someone to scrape me up. I was afraid to even try to move. I was afraid I wouldn't be able to move. I was sure she had snapped my spinal cord. I had this terrible pain. It turned out that she had spiked me in the rear end and gave me a knee in the shoulder when she tripped. I was too scared to realize that the pain meant that my spinal cord was intact."

Louise was staring hard at the ceiling, "In first-year university, I had to take a physiology lab. One of the experiments involved the nervous system of the frog. The instructor picked up this poor little frog and severed his spinal cord—just like that. It took everything I had not to get hysterical and attack the son of a bitch with my scalpel. I excused myself and left the room. I went into the lavatory and puked my guts out. I never went back to that physiology lab. The next day I marched into the Dean's office and changed my major to plant science. Every time I think of that frog, I can see a giant hand reaching out and snapping my spinal cord—just like that. Do you know how fragile the human body is?"

"I think that the human body is damned tough."

"I guess I've told you that story a hundred times." Louise said apologetically.

"Never so graphically."

"Sometimes I think that pain is the worst thing, but being a quadriplegic must be the worst thing."

"You bet."

"When you have fears you can sometimes deal with them by making detailed plans of action in the event that your fears are realized," Louise said, quoting the sports psychologist. "What would you do, Kay, if suddenly you became a quadriplegic?"

"I'd become an expert in oral sex."

"You're disgusting!" Nevertheless, Louise started to laugh. She stood up, reaching for her towel.

Kay stretched her legs out with a sigh. "I'm serious. Hell, what else could I do? I'd charge a hundred dollars a head—so to speak."

Louise had moved across the room and Kay had to raise her voice. "It would be a hell of a lot more fun than dispensing pills with my nose."

"As I said, you're disgusting." Louise stopped a few feet away. "Hey," she said suddenly, "my leg feels better."

"That's great. "

"Are you getting out now?"

"No." Kay began to paddle her legs. "Go ahead. Keep Terry company. I'll join you later."

"Don't be too long."

"I won't be." Kay was fixed on the motion of her legs. "I'm glad your legs feel better," she shouted after Louise. Louise, however, was out of earshot. "Your legs feel better and you've got me feeling as tight as a drum," she muttered to herself. She made a mental note not to indulge Louise's phobias again until after the Games. She was getting a mental image of the hapless frog and it made her cringe.

* * *

Terry and Louise had finished lunch and were dawdling over coffee when Kay finally arrived in the cafeteria. Terry had the latest copy of Track and Field propped on the table in front of him.

"She says you're afraid of speed," Terry greeted her.

"Who says I'm afraid of speed?" Kay deposited her broiled banyan, cheese sandwich, on the table and sat down opposite Louise.

"Ann Thomas. Louise says you're not afraid of anything," Terry challenged, "but this lady disagrees." He stabbed a finger at the headline. "She says so in an exclusive telephone interview with Jim Sparks." Terry moved his finger down the page, searching for the quote.

Kay noticed that he moved his lips as he read. "So read it to me."

"Yeah, yeah, I'm looking for it," Terry muttered. He continued to scan the pages, his eyes narrowing.

"Read the whole thing."

"The whole interview?"

"Yeah."

"OK." Terry sat back with a sigh.

Sparks: You haven't raced against Strachan in two years.

Thomas: Helsinki the World Championships was the last time, I think.

Sparks: You beat Strachan at Helsinki. In fact, she finished fourth, a good three minutes behind you.

Thomas: I don't remember. I remember that Parker was second. We ran the whole race, shoulder to shoulder. I was able to pull away finally in the last two hundred metres.

Sparks: Strachan has improved tremendously since Helsinki. Her 2:20:35 is the best ever for a woman in the marathon.

Thomas: That was at Boston.

Sparks: Were you surprised that Strachan set the record at Boston?

Thomas: Not really. Wells set her record there. Muller set her record there also.

Sparks: You ran Boston for the first time four years ago and haven't run it since.

Thomas: The hills—the downhill parts, I mean—are too hard on the legs. I had a lot of pain in my quads after Boston that year and I had blisters from slipping forward in my shoes. Boston is a great race. It's very historic and so forth but I don't think it's a good race for me.

Sparks: You were scheduled to run against Strachan in Chicago last fall. Everyone was predicting a great race and a record time. As it turned out, you turned up with an injury the week of the race and no one else really challenged Strachan. She won it in 2:25 and, after Boston, that seemed remarkably slow.

Thomas: 2:25 wasn't bad, considering the head-wind. Strachan might have been able to finish faster but, perhaps it would have been stupid to try. I know that she gives only what it takes to win. She wasn't pushed at Chicago.

Sparks: She wasn't pushed at Boston.

Thomas: I think Boston is a special case for her. The year I ran Boston, she tried to run from the front and it was a disaster for her. I think she has to prove something at Boston...."

"Get to the part about how I fear speed."

"Just wait." Terry paused to find his place. "Here, you'll like this."

Sparks: There were a few snide remarks following the Chicago Marathon. Some people were saying that the ankle injury was an excuse. The gist of the remarks was that, going into an Olympic year and after Strachan's performance in Boston, you didn't want to go head to head with her in Chicago. It would have been bad for you, psychologically, to be beaten in Chicago.

"Jim Sparks is vicious."

"Just wait."

Thomas: I've heard the remarks.

Sparks: Do they bother you?

Thomas: Not really. People always have to have something to say. Actually the ankle had been bothering me three or four weeks before Chicago. I hurt it in June at a 10K race in Manila. A month before Chicago, I stepped into a pothole during training and reinjured it. We were hoping it would be OK for Chicago but it didn't turn out that way. As I see it, all the pres-

sure in Chicago was on Strachan. I don't think that she had another sub:2:21 marathon in her at that stage and I had a chance. As it turned out, six weeks later, I ran a 2:22:10 in Sydney.

Sparks: What will the race in Montreal be like?

Thomas: It will be a tactical race. The course is pretty flat and the temperatures should be moderate. The conditions shouldn't favour anyone.

Sparks: They won't favour the runners who like hills, humidity and the like.

Thomas: No.

Sparks: In a recent interview, Strachan said that she had no plans to focus on any particular runner in Montreal.

Thomas: Obviously it depends on how the race develops. Unless she plans to take the lead and hold it—which I don't think she does—she will have to focus on what some of the other runners are doing.

Thomas: If Strachan fears anything, it's speed. She knows I've run a 2:22 marathon. Perhaps in some ways it was a tougher marathon than Boston.

Sparks: Your 2:22:10 in Sydney equals her 2:20:35 in Boston?

Thomas: Who can say? It's impossible to compare marathons. (Pause) Let's just say that we're both very fast.

Sparks: Strachan had to run the National Capital Marathon in Ottawa in order to qualify for the team. You were preselected. Will this affect Strachan's performance in Montreal?

Thomas: It will undoubtedly affect her training. I hear that she ran a very conservative race in Ottawa. Still, it has to be a disadvantage to run a qualifying marathon so close to the Olympics. I've been able to focus on the Montreal race and put in very high quality training because I didn't have to worry about the selection process.

Sparks:....

Kay waved Terry off rather wearily. "That's enough."

"She thinks you're scared of her. "

"She thinks I have a healthy respect for her speed and I do."

"Look at this." Terry flipped the magazine to show Kay the cover photo.

Kay viewed the cover dispassionately. "It's a nice shot."

"Pretty imposing, don't you think? Black singlet—Silver stripes—Matching shoes."

"She has a cute ass."

"Hell, you're no fun today." Terry pushed his chair back and stood up. "I'm wiped," he said. "I'm going to go home and take a long nap. Keep the mag."

"Thanks."

Louise had returned to her jaunty self. "So, are you all psyched out now?"

"Sure." Kay picked up the magazine and looked at it thoughtfully. "You know what's funny, Louise?"

"What?"

"The article was supposed to be about Thomas but all they talked about was me."

* * *

Tab was in bed when Kay got home that night, propped up against the pillows, reading a book.

"I thought you'd be somewhere with Esther," Kay said.

"Esther's out of town." Tab turned a page with a yawn. "She's giving a guest lecture at McMaster."

"Hot stuff." Kay disappeared into the kitchen and fixed a bowl of cereal.

Within minutes Tab appeared in the doorway, wrapping her robe around her. She poured a glass of milk and sat down at the table beside Kay.

"Hey," said Kay noticing the black arcs under Tab's eyes, "you don't look so good."

84

"I think I have a cold."

"Stay away from me." Kay looked at Tab apprehensively. "I don't need a cold right now."

"It's not that kind of cold. It's my sinuses. I think I'm allergic to something."

"You should have called me at Pop's. I would have brought something home."

"I didn't want to bother you." Tab set the milk aside. "I spent the afternoon in the archives. It's a little musty down there. I probably inhaled a swath of mould. "

"Maybe you should have some chicken soup. They say chicken soup is good for the sinuses."

"I've already had chicken soup. Esther brought some before she left town."

"Oh."

"You just missed her."

"Hell, I almost had a chance to meet her," said Kay, disappointed. "Or," she added, "maybe you're still not ready."

"What do you mean?"

"I'm a macho jock with a foul mouth. Remember?"

"Well, " said Tab, mildly triumphant, "you are going to get a chance to meet her. She's coming for dinner, Monday."

"Tab. I'm working Monday."

"Monday is Canada Day. When did Pop start opening on statutory holidays?"

"I forgot." Kay sat back with a sigh. "So, is she ready to meet me? "

"I've explained you to her."

"You've explained me to her?"

"Yes." Tab fingered the milk glass precisely. "I wanted her to be forewarned that, while you're basically a fine human being, she might find you—well—different."

"Different?" Kay looked at Tab in consternation.

"I told her that you are a bit conservative."

Kay could tell that Tab was hedging. "Conservative?" she asked sharply.

"All right," Tab confessed, "I told her that you're a redneck, that you have no interest in women's issues and that you're inclined to make derogatory remarks about minorities."

"Thanks."

"She's dying to meet you. She thinks you sound quaint."

"Quaint." Kay sighed deeply. "I've always wanted to be thought of as quaint."

"Quaint, eccentric—whatever," said Tab, trying to soften the blow.

"Eccentric." Kay lifted a skeptical eyebrow in Tab's direction. "Eccentric is Albert Einstein. Quaint means that you sit around in corners, sucking your toes."

"You'll like her."

"Hell," said Kay, a trifle miffed, "I'm a world-class athlete. There are people who would kill to meet me. Lots of them. This woman thinks I'm some sort of curiosity."

"She has no interest whatsoever in sports, Kay. You'll have to pretend that you're an ordinary person for the evening."

"Who else is coming to dinner?"

"Who do you want to come?"

"Louise"

"Louise can't come. I've already spoken to her."

"Damn!"

"I hear that you had coffee with your policewoman. Why don't you invite her?"

"Louise spilled her guts," said Kay, grimly. "So much for the sanctity of the Jacuzzi."

"Louise said that you invited her," Tab continued. "I'm surprised. I thought that you were eschewing entanglements until after the Games."

"She had a bad day. One of her bagladies died."

Tab nodded slowly, genuinely touched.

"You're a nice person, sometimes, Kay, and you try so hard not to be."

Kay caught the sincerity in Tab's voice and chose to ignore the latter part of the remark. "She came into Pop's again tonight. We were supposed to meet for coffee after work but she got tied up. She brought me a take-out. That was nice. "

"I think you should invite her to dinner, Monday."

"I don't know. I don't know if I want her to see that there's only one bedroom."

"There are two beds."

"I suppose." Kay paused and stared thoughtfully into space. "You know," she said finally, "it's funny. She seems so naive— for a cop—trusting, really soft. You'd think she should be running the Sunshine Day Care Center. But I saw her stand in the middle of a group of kids—she calls them kids. Actually they're vicious punks—and, suddenly, she had everything under control."

"I want you to invite her to dinner. I want to meet her. Do you think she's a feminist? Perhaps she'd like to speak to our group. We've never had a member of the police force as a speaker."

"Just wait a minute! " Kay looked at Tab sternly. "You took my friend Louise—a perfectly normal jock—and you turned her into a maniac. She's going around wearing a Women Don't Compete button."

"Women Shouldn't Compete," Tab corrected, "against women, in fine print."

"Against women—in fine print." Kay shook her head. "Maybe I'll invite Bill instead."

"Invite Mary."

"I'm not sure if I know her well enough." Kay's expression

87

was moody.

"You've had intimate contact with her hand. You've shared a vulnerable moment over a cup of coffee."

Tab looked especially determined.

Kay conceded with a sigh."Very well. I'll invite her. You've manoeuvred me into this, Tab."

"I'm not the one who ran down the street after her."

"Louise must take notes," said Kay, quietly exasperated. "I really don't need this right now—this thing with Mary." She reached down and pulled Terry's magazine out of her backpack."Do you see this woman, Tab?" She pointed to the picture on the cover.

"Ann Thomas?"

"Yeah." Kay flipped the magazine across the table. "She says I fear speed. She ran a 2:22 marathon in Sydney and she thinks I'm afraid of her. A 2:22 marathon against an insignificant headwind."

"Are you afraid of her?"

"No." Kay shook her head but Tab caught the familiar tightness around her mouth. "If she thinks she can beat me with speed," she muttered, "she's in for a surprise. She doesn't know how tough I can be."

"You're a hard woman." Tab stood up and picked up the dishes. She took them to the counter, rinsed them thoroughly and deposited them in the sink.

Kay sat at the table, staring at the magazine cover.

Tab went into the bathroom and began to brush her teeth.

Kay tossed the magazine into the corner and joined Tab at the sink. "Where's my toothbrush?"

"I threw it out," said Tab nonchalantly. "It was worn out. The bristles were sticking out in all directions."

"You threw out my toothbrush!"

"There's a new toothbrush for you right there on the top

shelf," Tab said calmly.

"It says it's firm. I don't like firm bristles. They hurt my gums."

"They massage your gums."

"It isn't red."

"What difference does that make?"

"I've always had a red toothbrush."

"Now you have a yellow toothbrush."

"Where's my old toothbrush?" Kay looked hopefully at the wastepaper basket.

"It is gone. It's down at the street. Tomorrow it will be picked up and taken to the city dump. It's gone, Kay."

Tab didn't wait for Kay to brush her teeth. She went to the bedroom and went directly to bed. Caesar was already curled up on the pillow.

Kay came into the room a few minutes later and sat down on her own bed.

"Sleep with me."

"I thought you weren't feeling well."

"I didn't ask you to have sex with me," said Tab. Her voice was muffled by the pillow. "I asked you to sleep with me."

"When you have sinus problems, you snore," Kay said, tiredly, "and you thrash around."

"I need you to keep me warm," Tab was petulant. "I don't like being chilled when I have sinus problems."

"All right."

Kay got up and climbed into Tab's bed. She eased her body against Tab's back. Caesar let his tail trail casually across her face. Kay spluttered and deposited him at the foot of the bed.

"How long is he going to live?"

"Don't say things like that."

"He doesn't understand a word I say."

"He senses things."

"So, how long?"

"Eighteen years."

"How old is he now?"

"He's six."

"Shit," Kay said with resignation.

Tab was wearing a nightshirt. Once in bed, it bunched up around her waist. In spite of its brevity, the garment annoyed Kay. She loved to feel all of Tab's skin against hers. It was soft and sensuous and it helped her sleep.

"Do you have to wear the nightshirt?"

"It keeps my back warm." Tab was beginning to mumble.

"That's what I'm here for—to keep your back warm."

"As soon as your arm falls asleep, you'll turn over and my back will be cold."

Kay accepted this bit of wisdom with a sigh. She pushed her hand up under the nightshirt and began to rub Tab's back in small, slow circles.

"That's nice."

"Does Esther rub your back?"

"Sometimes."

"I'm glad."

"Hm."

"You like having your back rubbed. I'm glad she rubs your back." Kay pressed her chin against Tab's shoulder so that she was talking directly into her ear. "They say that people need tactile stimulation. Otherwise, they curl up and die—like centipedes when you blast them with a can of Raid."

"I think you should sleep with Mary," said Tab, suddenly alert. She turned her head to look directly into Kay's eyes.

"I don't know her well enough,"

"You know her well enough to invite her to dinner. People sleep with total strangers, and sometimes find it very rewarding." Tab paused, stifling a yawn. "You need an adventure.

90

Whenever I see you lately—and it hasn't been nearly often enough— you seem spiritless. You've lost your spunk, Kay."

"I'm tired. I've been working hard."

"You've always worked hard. You've always needed a lot of stroking."

"Bill thinks I should spend some time in a sleep tank. He thinks I need mental freshness. He wants me to try it in Montreal. He has a friend...."

"You need a nice warm person who loves you, Kay."

"I don't have time."

"I know. With you, a courtship has to progress in neat, well-defined stages. Week one, it's candy and flowers; week two, it's a kiss at the door; a few months down the road, it's planning the silver and china and finding a suitable abode. If you insist upon doing things that way, you'll never have time. Sex isn't any better because you've waited six months."

"Don't remind me." Kay tossed her head back to avoid Tab's gaze.

Tab was silent for a moment. "I thought it was very sweet, the way you courted Bonnie," she said finally. "It was so old-fashioned, so rigid. It was marvellous. But, afterwards—once the relationship was established—you never seemed to have time for her. Afterwards, I wondered if the romantic preliminaries were expressions of romance or merely indicative of your penchant for scheduling, doing the right thing at the right time, pacing yourself."

"You know it wasn't that way."

Tab detected a catch in Kay's voice and she felt sorry. She turned over and gave Kay a quick hug.

"What's that for?"

" I'm sorry I haven't been around more often lately."

"There's nothing to be sorry about."

"You're my best friend. I've neglected you because I'm involved in a relationship."

"That's normal."

"Still, it's not right—especially not after the National Capital.I know how morose you can be when you're recovering from a big race."

"It wasn't like that this time. I didn't put out enough to get a downer."

"You've been morose." Tab turned abruptly, pulling Kay's arm around her waist. "Sleep with Mary."

"You think all I need is a good night in the sack?"

"Companionship, Kay. Stroking."

Kay settled in against Tab's back. "I used to think about sex all the time When I was eighteen. I must have masturbated six times a day." She paused, staring dully into the darkness. "Lately, I don't think I've masturbated in weeks, maybe not in months. Sometimes, when you don't think about sex, you forget that you want it. Then, when you think about it and want it, it's not there."

She stopped talking, waiting for a response but Tab said nothing. "One shouldn't even think about it, "she continued, "unless there is a beautiful, naked woman right there in your bed." Kay pressed against Tab rather hopefully. She was greeted by a resounding snore.

She disentangled her arm from Tab's waist and turned over onto her back, lacing her fingers together behind her head. She was thinking about having sex with Mary when she drifted off and hoped that she would dream about it.

Instead, she dreamed about racing against Ann Thomas. The venue wasn't Montreal or Boston or even Tokyo. They were running down a cow path. Thomas weighed three hundred pounds and carried a pail cf water in each hand. She lumbered along, huffing and puffing under her burden.

Kay ran past her and shot out of sight.

Chapter 12

That Wednesday, Kay invited Mary to dinner. Mary was scheduled to work until ten but, after a quick call to the station, managed to rearrange her hours.

"The Sergeant says he can use me for traffic control that day," she told Kay upon returning. "He's assigned me to Ontario Place."

Kay pretended to concentrate on a prescription for Jean's benefit. "So, you get to stand around for hours, waving your arms."

"Yes," Mary said with a grimace. "It's boring but it'll get me off duty by six."

"Then we can expect you for seven."

* * *

Kay met Mary at the submarine shop across the street at nine for coffee. It was then that Mary asked Kay if she could run with her.

"You want to run with me?" Kay struggled valiantly to suppress the incredulity in her tone.

"I thought it might be fun," Mary said innocently. "Besides, I'd like to see you sometime when we're not both working."

"Yeah," Kay agreed nervously, "you've been spending so much time at Pop's lately, Jean probably thinks you're a drug addict."

"So, what do you say?" Mary asked brightly. "I was on the

93

cross-country team in high school. I haven't run competitively since then but I'm in good shape. I do a lot of walking."

"How fast can you run?"

"Between seven and seven-and-a-half, I think. I score in the top twenty per cent on my annual fitness reviews."

"That's good, very good. You should enter some of the local 10K's. You might do OK."

"I'll think about it." Mary reached across the table and tapped Kay on the forearm. "So, what do you say? Can I run with you?"

"I don't know." Kay stared at the table. "I mean, I run pretty fast. Even when I'm running slow, it's pretty fast."

"How fast?"

"Six-fifteen. That's about as slow as I go."

"Oh." Mary picked up her serviette, then dropped it into her lap. She made a pretence of folding it.

"I wouldn't want you to rip up your achilles or anything, trying to keep up," said Kay, a little desperate at Mary's obvious disappointment. "I mean, it takes years to shave a minute off your time. The muscles can handle the load a little faster maybe but all the changes in the cardiovascular system—all that takes a lot longer." Kay finally realized that she was babbling into the tablecloth. She raised her head, meeting Mary's gaze hesitantly. "I'm sorry," she said. "I guess you weren't looking for a lecture in physiology."

"It's OK," Mary said softly. "I do understand. I guess it wouldn't be appropriate to ask Larry Holmes to go a few rounds either."

"No, no, it's not that," Kay assured hastily. "Look, I'd like to run with you." She paused then said with conviction. "Tomorrow. Mount Pleasant Cemetery. Eleven a.m. "

"Mount Pleasant Cemetery?"

"Yeah, Mount Pleasant Cemetery. Every morning I do eight

94

to ten miles. I end up with a warm-down in the cemetery. I'll meet you there after my workout and we'll do a couple of easy miles. It's a nice place for a leisurely run."

"Doesn't anyone object?"

"Why?" Kay looked at Mary blankly. "They're all dead."

"I mean, the authorities, the caretakers, the bereaved." Mary's lips parted in a smile. Kay, who thought she had never seen Mary really smile, was captivated.

"Oh, no," Kay said sheepishly. "I run on the paths. Well," she confessed, "most of the time I run on the paths. Sometimes, if no one's looking, I run on the grass. Just on the edges, you know. I try not to run over anybody's final resting place."

"Be careful that you don't run into the mounted police."

Kay wanted to say that she wouldn't mind as long as the officer was a woman and as pretty as Mary Johnson. But the submarine shop was crowded and noisy. The sentiment deserved a better atmosphere. Besides, Mary was glancing at her watch and that meant it was time to go."

Kay followed her out onto the street and said good night at the corner.

Chapter 13

Kay ran with Mary on Wednesday, Thursday and Friday. The seven-minute pace which Mary set on the first day seemed like a walk to Kay. By Friday, however, she sensed that Mary had picked up the pace slightly and told her so. They were sitting under a tree in Mount Pleasant Cemetery. "I think that was a 6:58."

"How do you know?"

"Hey," Kay chided, "I'm an old pro at this. Bill says I have the best pacing sense he's ever seen. He thinks I'm wasting my money on a stopwatch."

"But you wear one when you're racing."

"Sure, it makes me look glamorous." Kay nudged Mary's arm. "Come on, let me see your watch. It says 6:58, doesn't it?"

"I don't know. I didn't set it."

"Yes, you did. I saw you."

"OK," Mary admitted, "you're right. It says 6:58."

"See." Kay sat back, triumphant.

"I'll bet you peeked."

"I did not."

"How do you know we ran a mile?"

"I counted the steps."

"We were talking. How did you count the steps?"

"I do it all the time." Kay rested her head against the tree trunk. "I don't know how. I guess it's automatic. My brain takes over and does it for me. We runners are very talented people."

"So I see."

"Yeah." Kay paused, frowning. "Most people don't realize that, you know. They think you became a runner because you were too short for basketball or had lousy eye-hand coordination or something like that."

"Do you have lousy eye-hand coordination."

Kay looked at Mary with a smile. "As a matter of fact, I do." She knew that Mary was teasing. It surprised her that she rather enjoyed it. "And I probably am too short for basketball," she added.

"Spud Webb is only 5'6"."

"But he has good eye-hand coordination." Kay shrugged. "It's funny, I hold the world record for the marathon and people still ask me what my favourite sport is—people who should know better."

"What is your favourite sport?"

"Hopscotch." Kay turned to give Mary a look of mock exasperation but the next thing she knew they were lying on the grass together, kissing.

* * *

"How did your run go today?" Tab asked Kay later that evening. Esther was out of town again and Tab had a stack of cookbooks spread over the kitchen table.

"Great. I feel good. My intervals are right where I want them."

"I was referring to your run with Mary."

"That was great too. She did a sub-seven today."

"Is she going with you tomorrow?"

"I'm going to Kleinburg tomorrow and she has to work."

"I thought Bill was cutting down on your mileage."

"He is." Kay opened the refrigerator door and began to rum-

97

mage through the shelves. "Tomorrow will be an easy fifteen miles."

"There's shredded wheat in the cupboard."

"What's there to put on it?" Kay took the milk from the refrigerator and put it on the counter.

"Peaches."

"Canned or fresh?"

"Canned. There aren't any fresh peaches at this time of year."

Kay opened the cupboard door and took out the shredded wheat. She stared at the peaches for a long time, trying to decide if it was worth the effort to find the can opener and open the can. It wasn't. She closed the cupboard door and brought the shredded wheat to the table with the milk.

"Why do you do it that way?" Tab's brow was furrowed over a picture of roast beef.

"Do what, what way?"

"Bring the milk to the table? Why don't you pour the milk on the cereal at the counter and put the milk back into the refrigerator? Now you'll have to get up again to put the milk away."

"Because I won't know if I have the right amount of milk until I start eating. If I don't have the right amount I'll have to get up again anyway." Kay took a bite of the cereal then, to prove her point, dribbled a little more milk over the biscuit.

Tab shook her head.

Kay took another bite. "I kissed her."

"Really?" Tab looked at Kay with interest. "Well, I'm very proud of you." There was a hint of surprise in her voice.

"Right there in Mount Pleasant Cemetery." Kay began to toy absently with her cereal. "It's very nice in Mount Pleasant Cemetery."

"Mount Pleasant Cemetery is very nice."

"We ended up having a real necking session."

98

"Kay, I can't believe this is you talking! A necking session in a public place!"

"There was a bush," Kay temporized, "and some sort of mausoleum."

"Still, it sounds terribly spontaneous."

"I don't know if I like being spontaneous. I like to be sure about these things."

"Kay!"

"When you're too casual, people can get hurt."

"Did you enjoy it?"

Kay looked at Tab suspiciously, but Tab looked perfectly serious. "Yeah, I guess I did."

"Did she enjoy it?"

"I think so." She wanted to tell Tab how good Mary's breasts had felt but she couldn't find the right words and she was afraid if she used the wrong words they would sound lewd. She wanted to share, with Tab, Mary's sweet sadness—the melancholy that lingered even in the laughter. But she couldn't do justice to the feeling and thinking of it depressed her. So, she said nothing.

"She's a nice person," she said aloud. "I don't want her to get hurt. I don't want her to expect too much of me."

"In case you can't deliver."

"I guess so."

"Kay, no woman in her right mind would base her future on a pleasant interlude in Mount Pleasant Cemetery."

"I don't know. Look at Debbie. Remember that woman she met in the bar? She was crushed."

"Most women are more sophisticated than Debbie. They realize that a friendly gesture—a brief period of intimacy—doesn't guarantee a twenty-year commitment. It's part of the freedom of the modern lesbian, Kay, to love and make love and enjoy it and," Tab concluded with a small shrug, "when the physical intimacy ends, to be friends—perhaps on a much higher level."

"What would you do if you were passionately in love with a woman and she led you down the garden path?"

"I've been passionately in love with dozens of women, Kay, and I've never been led down the garden path."

"What if once, just once, you were led down the garden path?"

"I suppose I'd feel slightly betrayed."

"Betrayed?"

"If I felt someone had been dishonest, I'd feel betrayed—as a person."

"But not crushed?"

"Of course not."

"Two years ago," Kay challenged. "Remember? The graduate student from Cambridge. Prudence Greenridge."

"Prudence Greenham," Tab corrected.

"Whatever." Kay waved the correction aside impatiently. "You didn't eat for a week."

"If you love someone, you may experience a brief period of grieving when the relationship ends," Tab said evenly. "That is quite different from being crushed or devastated. Being crushed or devastated is the outcome of a certain heterosexual conditioning which dictates that we base our hopes for the future and our value as persons on the success or failure of the love-sex relationship."

"I take it that the group doesn't approve of twenty-year relationships."

"Of course. If they work." Tab frowned. "Kay, you're obtuse. There are plenty of good twenty-year relationships. They are not, however, necessarily based on sexual or domiciliary exclusiveness."

"Hm." Kay shook her head. "I'm definitely obtuse."

100

"And a slave to mainstream social conditioning."

"And a slave to mainstream sexual conditioning."

"Social—but that too."

Kay digested this information for a moment, then decided to change the subject. "By the way, I got your Olympic tickets today."

"Good." Tab shifted rather uncomfortably but Kay did not notice.

"I've been asking Bill for them for weeks. He's had them locked in a drawer at home."

"I suppose he was afraid that you would lose them."

"Probably." Kay reached for her backpack and removed the folder. "They're the best you can get. They'll get you into all the finals—whatever you want."

"Thank you." Tab took the folder, examined it briefly, then set it aside.

Kay leaned over the table to look at the cookbook. "So, what are we having for dinner, Monday?"

"Shrimp in garlic butter sauce, rolls, salad. I haven't decided on the vegetables yet."

"How about cauliflower au gratin," said Kay, naming her favourite.

"Cauliflower au gratin does not go well with shrimp, Kay. I was considering green beans—French style of course"

"Terrific. What's for dessert?"

"Bavarian cream."

"Do you know how to make all this stuff?" Kay asked respectfully.

"Of course. It's easy to cook if you follow the instructions." Tab turned a page in the cookbook, pausing over a recipe for rice pilaf. "I'm going to need you here, Monday. I don't want you running in at the last minute."

"Need me for what?"

"To set the table, to cut up vegetables for the salad, entertain the guests, give me moral support."

"You're nervous about this, aren't you? We've had people for dinner hundreds of times. You've never wanted me near the kitchen before. You always chase me out of the house to get butter or something."

"I've never cooked for Mary before. Naturally, I'm nervous. I'm always nervous when I cook for someone I don't know."

"Mary eats at the deli every night. She must have a cast-iron stomach. Her taste buds are probably so screwed up that she can't tell tea from coffee. She'll be grateful for the chance to have a hot meal cooked by someone other than Gus Antopolis."

"Food is symbolic, Kay. Making an effort for guests is a gesture of friendship."

"I'll bet you're trying to impress Esther," said Kay smugly.

"I don't need to impress Esther."

"Then why are you taking gourmet cooking classes?"

"Louise told you!"

"Who else?"

"Cooking is something I enjoy," Tab said, a trifle defensive. "The classes have nothing to do with impressing Esther."

"Pleasing her then?"

"Perhaps."

"I thought that you once said that attempting to impress or please someone," said Kay, putting the emphasis on the or, "is a cardinal sign of ego weakness." She paused, trying to recapture the words exactly. "Ego weakness in women uncertain of their personal worth."

"Why do you always remember the wrong things?" Tab asked irritably.

"I think ego weakness was the first phrase you learned when you joined the group. You parroted it at me for a week. You said that I at least had no ego problems, that I wouldn't

102

think of lifting a finger to please anyone." Kay was definitely pleased with herself.

Tab, who normally would have praised Kay for even a garbled version of the group credo, seemed deflated. "It's something I have to overcome," she said quietly.

"Well, don't make it sound as if you're hooked on cocaine." Kay caught Tab's expression of disapproval and tried to be more serious. "So, what is wrong with pleasing people?"

"There's nothing wrong with pleasing people.It's needing to please people that's the problem. It implies that you're afraid to let your person stand by itself in a relationship."

Kay tilted her chair back and ran Tab's words through her mind for a few moments. "I think that what you're saying is a bunch of bull."

"I can't stand it when you're so intellectual." Tab's voice had taken on a hard edge. "Why can't we have a sane, sharing discussion without it ending with one of your totally judgmental pronouncements?"

"Judgmental pronouncements." Kay shook her head."I think you're just so goddamned stupid to torture your soul over a pot of green beans and," she added, taking a deep breath, "trying to disguise the fact with a lot of high-flown shit doesn't help."

"Language is important. Language reflects thinking. Language creates thinking. And, while we're on the topic, I hope that you can survive through dinner, Monday, without exhausting your vocabulary of four-letter words."

"I thought I wasn't supposed to dwell upon pleasing anyone."

"You're not." Tab's words were more deliberate. "You're a well-educated woman. Occasionally—when you think no one's looking—you even read the odd decent piece of literature.I think that you diminish yourself when you resort to locker-

103

room language."

Kay considered this briefly, then said," Remember how you always say that social scientists use weird words in order to convey thoughts more precisely?"

"Yes."

"Well, for an athlete, fuck is the most beautifully precise word invented. It comes right out of your heart. You wrench it right out of your gut, the way you tear out of yourself everything else that's worthwhile." Kay's tone rose in intensity, then dropped abruptly. "Shit is a close second."

"That's good." Tab looked at Kay, nodding with surprised respect. "Why haven't you done that before?"

"Done what?"

"Relate your language to your inner being, to the intensity of your athletic person? I've always thought that you were just being careless."

"I've never really thought of it before. I guess all my brains are in my slow-twitch fibres."

Tab was silent and Kay imagined that she was angry. "Are you mad at me?" she ventured tentatively.

"No."

"Good." Kay breathed a sigh of relief. "Bill phoned me at Pop's tonight. The shoe guys have been calling again. He says if I win the gold medal, they'll make me rich."

"If you endorse their product."

"Yeah."

"Are you going to do it?"

"I don't know." Kay surprised herself with the readiness of her answer. "Sometimes after those evenings at Pop's, after training all day, I think I deserve to be rich."

"There's plenty of money to be made in road racing."

Kay sighed, "but it's not as secure as an endorsement."

"After the Olympics you can do whatever you want."

104

"If I win the gold medal, I can do whatever I want—road race and take my purse without a twinge. If I don't win this time out, it's another four years of cold-water flats and Pop's."

"What do you want to do?"

"I want to road race. I want to train hard. I want to pick my races and run quality times."

"You do that now."

"And I want to have my evenings free."

"To do what?"

"To rest."

"You can rest after you're dead."

Kay ignored the remark and said wistfully. "I'd like to know what it's like not to roll out of bed at six, knowing that I'm going to be on my feet until nine p.m. Bill's cut back on my training," she said quietly, almost to herself. "The last four years, we've worked harder than anybody. We've done more miles and better speedwork. I know that we had to taper after Ottawa but, normally, we would have picked it up a little more at this stage. Bill thinks we're at a critical point. He thinks I'm on the edge right now. He thinks if we push too hard I could end up on the wrong side—stale."

"I thought that your training was going well."

"It is," Kay said, a little fretfully. "Putting in the miles is important though—psychologically. Bill thinks we should take a gamble. He wants to blow the bundle on high quality work from here on in."

"You trust Bill, don't you?"

"Yeah, I do. He's always been right before. He's kept me away from everything from bicarb loading to DMSO. I know he's right. We've just never done it this way before."

"Well." Tab yawned. "I doubt if Bill is gambling. He has all the daring of a three-toed sloth. You're his star. His sun rises and sets on you. He would no more take a chance with your

105

training, than change his bow tie. Sometimes I think he's inside your skin. If he were half-way to the moon, he would have a finger on your pulse. If he wasn't such a plodder, I'd think he was Machiavellian."

"He looks after me. He makes life a lot easier for me."

Tab was about to say something but Kay looked curiously vulnerable and she changed her mind.

"It's a good team, you and Bill," she said simply.

* * *

She didn't ask Kay to sleep with her that night and Kay didn't make any overtures. She thought that Kay might be restless, as she often was in the final stages of preparation for a major race. But Kay fell asleep quickly and slept noiselessly.

Tab finally drifted off at three a.m. She woke briefly at six when she heard the toilet flush. A few minutes later, the apartment door opened and closed.

Tab turned over and fell back to sleep until ten.

Chapter 14

"You said you wouldn't need me until five," Kay said in response to Tab's fretful query as to her whereabouts.

"I need you to go to the store for me." Tab was searching frantically for her wallet.

"What do you want? I have money." Kay began to rifle through her pockets. She tossed the crumpled bills onto the counter and counted out the change in the palm of her hand.

"Well," she said finally, "if what you want doesn't cost more than eighteen and a quarter, we've got it made."

"I need a dozen dinner rolls. "

"I thought you were making dinner rolls."

"They didn't turn out well."

"Were they gummy in the middle?"

"No, I burned them." Tab turned her attention back to the stove. "Get two dozen of Pete Capucci's crusty rolls—the small ones."

"Do you want anything else?"

"No."

Tab was concentrating on the steaming pots. Kay shrugged and started toward the door.

"Don't dawdle," Tab called after her.

* * *

Kay was sitting at the kitchen table when Esther arrived. She got up to answer the door but Tab got there first. Esther gave Kay a smile and kissed Tab on the mouth. Kay noticed, to her amusement, that Tab was fluttering.

The first thing she noticed about Esther was the beautiful, liquid-brown eyes. They flickered over her with casual thoroughness as her hands found Tab's rear end.

"I've heard all about you," Esther said as Tab performed the introductions. She kissed Kay on the cheek. It was, Kay decided, one of those feminist-lesbian rituals.

"That's too bad," Kay said and the brown eyes laughed again.

* * *

"We need to find a way," Esther said over dessert, "to let young lesbian women explore their sexuality without raising the spectre of recruitment."

"Recruitment?" Kay asked.

"Yes. Whenever we hold an educational or attempt to form support groups for teen-age lesbians, the public assumes that we're trying to recruit young women for our own sexual purposes."

"Women from small towns often tell me how lucky I was to grow up in Toronto," Tab said with a sigh. "The truth of the matter is, I might as well have grown up in Wawa. At sixteen, I was too young to go to the bars and the women's groups were afraid of me." Dinner had been a great success and Tab was now relaxed and talkative. "I was seventeen when I started university," she continued. "I thought that being a university student would make a difference. It didn't."

"She had a real baby face," Kay said.

"Finally, I had to resort to lying about my age. I pretended I was nineteen."

"Yeah," Kay said soberly, "and finally an eighteen-year-old took her to bed. The kid thought she was dealing with an older woman."

108

"When did you have your first sexual encounter, Kay?"

"What!" Kay looked at Esther, startled.

Esther assumed that Kay had misunderstood the question.

"With a woman," she added.

"Oh." Kay swallowed a little harder than she had intended. "I didn't know there was any other kind." She meant to drop the subject there but Esther was looking at her expectantly. They were all looking at her. "I was fifteen," she said hurriedly. "Fifteen is such a nondescript age, you know. When you're fourteen, you're a real teenager. Sixteen, wow! But, fifteen...."

"How did it happen?"

"She was my best friend. We were on the cross-country team together. We were always fooling around—you know, wrestling, trying to see how far we could bend our fingers back, doing the kinds of things kids do at that age. One day we were fooling around on her bed and"—she shrugged, trying to appear casual— "it happened."

"You're blushing."

"I'm not blushing, Tab."

"She always blushes when she tells this story," Tab said happily. "She can relate any other experience she's had in shocking detail and not blink an eye."

"I guess I remember how I felt then," Kay said lamely.

"How did you feel?" Esther persisted.

"Like blushing." Kay stared at the table. "We didn't even take our clothes off. Afterwards, we pretended that nothing had happened. But," she said wistfully, "we never wrestled on her bed again."

"I was eighteen," Esther said after a lengthy pause. "I was taking art lessons with a vital, older woman. She was married and that was very positive. We were able to enjoy our encounters—and the friendship—without burdening each other."

"It doesn't sound as if your heart was leaping out of your

109

throat with passion," Kay scoffed. After her own, very personal confession, she felt cheated.

"On the contrary. I was an adoring pupil. I worshipped the woman. She was a wonderful teacher and," Esther added with a twinkle in her eye, "if you're wondering about the sex, it was magnificent. The woman was a virtuoso, totally in command of the situation. It was a hopelessly easy initiation."

"I'll bet you even took your clothes off."

"Every time."

Mary had been listening to the conversation with interest but without comment. "I was twenty-six," she said suddenly.

"You sound as if you're apologizing," Esther said.

"I think it's harder when you're older."

"Societal overlay," Esther said briefly. She put her spoon aside. "Excellent, Tab."

"Thank you."

"Adults in our society are supposed to be sexually active," said Mary.

"Exactly," said Esther. "And, as we grow older, our sense of who we are strengthens. It becomes more difficult for our bedmates to satisfy our ego perceptions in the sexual context."

"Because, in our society, sex has become such an important part of our self-image," Tab added. "I wonder how the cave women ever did it."

* * *

"Well, what did you think of her?" Tab asked when the evening was over.

Mary had left a few minutes earlier and Esther had gone down to her car, laden with Tab's books. That, Kay surmised, meant that Tab wouldn't be around for a few days.

"I think she's gorgeous." Kay helped herself to a stray cracker. "She's so gorgeous, she should be arrested for contributing to everybody's delinquency."

110

"Apart from the obvious?" Tab's voice was cool but Kay thought she looked proud.

"She's OK—as feminists go. She has a sense of humour. I like that. You don't often see a feminist with a sense of humour."

Tab looked at Kay thoughtfully. "Considering what goes on in the world, it's a wonder one ever meets a feminist with a sense of humour. I think I'll accept your comments as complimentary though. I should give you credit for setting aside your preconceived notions long enough to concede that the woman might have some saving graces."

"I managed to shuck them for the evening."

"You were good." Tab paused. "I liked Mary. She seems like a very solid woman. I thought I detected a rather pleasant nurturing quality about her."

"Funny, I always think of her as being a little fragile."

"She's strong enough to let her fragility show," Tab said briskly. "I'm glad she agreed to speak to the group." Tab packed up the leftovers as she spoke, carefully wrapping each item in plastic wrap. "Why didn't you go home with her?"

"She has to get up really early tomorrow. She's going on a retreat for the rest of the week—some sort of educational at the police academy."

"When will you see her again?"

"Saturday. She's coming to Kleinburg with me."

"That's good. You can spend the whole day together."

"Carol Hartly," Kay said suddenly.

"Who? "

"Carol Hartly—the girl on the cross-country team. I haven't thought about her in years. "Kay leaned against the counter, smiling a little sadly. "Hey," she said gently, "do you remember the name of that older woman?"

"Her name was Barbara Knight," said Tab without a mo-

111

ments hesitation.

"Fifteen years old," Kay continued wistfully. "When you're fifteen, you think you're an old lady. You think you know everything there is to know. You think you know how it's going to feel. Hell," she took a deep breath. "It's sort of like knowing you're going to have breasts. When it happens, it's a lot different than you thought it was going to be. We were just kids and we were afraid to take our clothes off. It would have been so innocent...."

Tab had stopped fussing and was regarding her seriously but Kay didn't notice. "Everybody conspires to keep you ignorant," she murmured. "Even what they do teach you isn't much help. I got great marks in Hygiene in junior high school.I had the parts of the female anatomy down cold. Then, suddenly, you're in bed with a woman for the first time.You're in a passionate embrace. She's asking you to stroke her clitoris and you can't find the damned thing."

"You couldn't find Carol Hartly's clitoris?" said Tab.

"I don't know if Carol Hartly knew she had a clitoris. I was speaking generally."

"Hm." Tab looked at Kay thoughtfully. She wanted to suggest that, perhaps, Kay wasn't speaking so generally and she wasn't sure if she was thinking about Carol Hartly. "It's hard growing up," she said simply.

"Are you ready, Tab?" Esther's voice floated up the stairs.

"I'm ready."

Esther appeared in the doorway, looking fresh in spite of having climbed three flights of steps. She put her arm around Tab and spoke to Kay. "I hope you don't mind," she said, "but I'm going to take this woman away."

Kay shrugged. "It's OK. She's getting on my nerves, gift-wrapping the leftovers."

Tab hovered in the doorway. "Use the leftovers tomorrow."

112

Esther kissed Kay on the cheek once again and said she hoped that Kay would come to a meeting. Kay lied and said she would while Tab shook her head in admonishment behind Esther's back.

Kay could hear Tab's voice as the door closed. The voices gradually faded and the outside door snapped open and shut abruptly.

Suddenly it was very quiet.

Kay reached into the refrigerator, got out a jar of pickles. She walked around the apartment, crunching absently on a dill. The bedroom door was closed. Kay recalled that Caesar had been banished from the living room after snatching a canape. She opened the door and looked in.

Caesar was stretched over the arm of a chair like a beanbag, his head hanging inertly. He was snoring. Kay closed the door and returned to the living room.

She picked up the telephone and called Mary. "I just wanted to see that you got home OK," she said when Mary answered the phone. "All those crazies out on the street...you never know....Yeah? I'm glad....Yeah. Tab's a great cook. I made the salad....sometimes Tab can be really fussy about the kitchen....yeah....She thinks I make a mess....not really....she's just particular....yeah...well. I just wanted to make sure you got home all right....good, good. I'll be working pretty hard....have a good time in Aylmer. I'll see you Saturday....yeah...I'll pick you up at nine."

Kay hung up the receiver and stared blankly at the telephone for a moment. Then she went over and switched on the television set. Bob was vilifying the Blue Jays bullpen. "Going to these guys is like using kerosene to douse your hibachi," he was saying. Kay shook her head as Roy Lee served up a two-run homer.

Kay sat down in Tab's chair and put her feet up on the otto-

113

man. Caesar had come alive suddenly and was scratching at the door. Kay tried to ignore him but the plaintive cries and the orange paw waving frantically under the door caused her to relent.

She opened the door. Caesar went directly to his food dish and waited patiently. Kay guessed that, in the excitement of the evening, Tab had forgotten to feed him.

"I don't have time to warm up your slop," Kay told him. "You'll have to eat this." She poured some kibble into the dish and set it on the floor.

Caesar complained, but weakly.

Kay returned to sit in her chair and, presently, Caesar joined her. He perched on the arm of the chair, linked his arm through hers and gazed at her fondly. Kay gave him a grudging pat.

When Kay woke at three, the television screen was blank. Caesar was stretched out across her knees, calmly washing his ears.

Chapter 15

"Did Tab tell you what happened at the meeting on Tuesday?" Louise asked Kay as she joined her for lunch on the following Thursday.

"I haven't seen Tab since Monday." They were dining with Bill and Kay's attention was focussed on Bill's bow tie which bobbed up and down with each swallow.

"The group is sending a delegation to demonstrate at the Olympics."

"That's crazy." Kay started to laugh. "The security will be so tight, they won't get within miles of the stadium."

"That's why they're demonstrating along the marathon route."

Bill's ears picked up at the mention of the race. "Who's demonstrating along the marathon route?"

"It's just a bunch of crazy women, some group Tab belongs to," Kay explained. "They think that competition among women is detrimental to the advancement of women and so on."

"That's nonsense." Bill began to carve up his steak with great vigour. "Competition is a great thing for the girls. When you have great competition, everyone is interested. It makes more chances for the young kids. They see that sports can be a good thing for them, a real career."

"The women feel that rewarding the top athletes is a form of tokenism," Louise explained. "You know, hand out a few morsels, just enough to keep women thinking that they can improve their lot within the system when, in fact, they should be ripping it up by the roots. They feel that, ultimately, competitive aggression may inhibit the kinds of accomplishments that can be achieved through cooperation."

"It takes aggression to do things in the world."

"These women feel that aggression is a male way of dealing with problems. Ultimately, it may not be good for women."

"That is the excuse people used to use for why women should not run the marathon," Bill said impatiently. "They said that it would make women like men. I think they should let women be what they want to be."

"I think you should speak to the group, Bill," Kay teased. "And I always thought you were such a chauvinist."

"I am not a chauvinist." Bill looked at Kay in surprise. "I've always coached the women. People ask me why when I have the choice. I'll tell you, the women are a lot easier to motivate. They work harder and," he sank his fork into a piece of steak, "they do what you tell them to do."

"I think you just flunked the test." Kay shook her head. "You were doing great, right up until the end. So," she said, turning to Louise, "are you going to be waving a banner at the twenty-mile mark?"

"I abstained from the vote." Louise opened her sandwich and looked at the contents suspiciously. "This isn't real ham."

"You abstained?"

"Sure. I may agree with the women in principle, Kay. But it would look a little silly, don't you think, to compete in the 1500 then go out and demonstrate against the marathon?"

"It would look pretty silly."

"Tab abstained too."

"Really?"

"She felt that it would be unfair to single out a particular group of athletes. She felt that the public might misinterpret the gesture."

"And think that you were a group of radical feminist anti-marathoners."

"Right."

"That would be very limiting."

"She said that she would go," Louise continued. "However, she doesn't plan to demonstrate. She said that she would stand along the route only because Esther is involved."

"Not because she supports the cause."

"These people aren't dangerous, are they?" Bill looked concerned.

"Only to themselves."

"Bunch of tomfoolery." Bill sniffed. "I always thought Tab had some horse sense. When she was a little kid doing the hurdles, she had some sense." After making this speech, he disappeared back into his steak.

Kay picked up her coffee cup and, for a few minutes, they ate in silence. "Do you think she's happy?" she asked Louise suddenly.

"Sure." Louise shrugged. "Don't you?"

"I don't know." Kay sighed. "Sometimes she seems so remote. We've been friends for years. But, lately, we seem so far apart."

Louise shook her head soothingly. "She has a lot on her mind these days. She's involved in a very intense relationship. She's preparing to go to North Borneo in September. She's teaching a class in the summer session."

"She hasn't talked much about North Borneo lately," Kay murmured, "and I didn't even know that she had a class this summer."

"I suppose you think that you haven't been preoccupied lately." Louise wagged an accusing finger. "I lapped you twice on

117

the track this morning and you didn't even notice. I've heard that things are happening with you too."

"Things?"

"Tab tells me that you and Mary are becoming a very hot item."

"Hm." Kay glanced at Bill who was trying to pretend that he wasn't listening.

"Why don't you move in with her and let me have your apartment?"

"I really haven't thought about the apartment." Kay looked subdued. "Maybe Tab will want it when she comes back. Maybe I want it myself."

"Tab will probably move in with Esther." Louise tapped Kay on the forearm pointedly. "And you, what would you want to stay there for? Once the Olympics are over, you'll be able to buy half of Rosedale."

"Rosedale," Kay murmured. "Actually, I was planning on moving into Tab's mother's place with Caesar."

"I think Caesar's moving in with Esther."

"Oh." Kay shrugged. "Well, he hasn't said a lot to me lately either."

"You've got to start preparing yourself," Louise said seriously. "After you win the gold medal, they'll be throwing money at you. They'll want you for commercials, speaking engagements. It'll make the offers you get now look like pretty small potatoes."

"Yeah," Kay said wryly, "I could advertise butter like Gaeten Boucher. I could dress up like a rutabaga and do the Ontario Foodlands promo at the Ex."

"You could get a terrific house. You could have your own quarter-mile track. I could move in over the garage."

"Are you really desperate for a place to live, Louise?"

"I'm getting a little old to be living with my parents, Kay.
118

It's cheap but not convenient."

"Ask your Dad to buy you a house. He yanks more teeth than any other dentist in Toronto."

"He's already financing my master's program." Louise said with a grimace. "And I may need him for another four years. I'm probably not going to win a medal—not this time around—and I'm not going to have people throwing money at me."

"If you think that way, I'm sure you won't win a medal."

"The East Germans are going to sweep the medals, Bill. Even the Americans are conceding that."

"The East German girls might get sick or throw a hamstring or fall down. Who knows what will happen."

"It's just terrific when your coach thinks that you'll have a chance only if the rest of the field falls down," Louise said, laughing. "Excuse me," she said, "I need another donut. Does anyone else want anything?"

"I'll have another coffee, thanks." Bill began to rummage for change.

"It's on me, Coach."

"She's the best middle-distance runner in Canada," Bill told Kay when Louise was out of earshot. "She has met her potential. What more can be asked?"

"People can dream, Bill."

"Sure, people can dream. She's happy with her progress now. She's going to the Olympics. She should enjoy that as the big moment in her life. I never went to the Olympics."

Kay studied Bill gravely.

"It's funny, she said, "the way you handle Louise is so different from the way you handle me."

"You have not reached your potential," he said calmly. "There is still a lot in you to dredge out. You will be the first woman to run a 2:19 marathon. A 2:15 is definitely within your reach. I even dare to think that you can do better."

119

"Maybe Louise would do better if you said something like that."

"She knows that our expectations are realistic. In the back of her mind, she knows that. She would like to surprise me. When she dreams, it is that she is just a little better than I think she is." He shrugged, without apology. "She will do her best in Montreal. She will take, maybe, a half-second off her best time."

"Why can't she take another half-second off next year and another the year after that?"

"She has limits. You don't have such limits. Sometimes I see you running to the moon."

"You're such a bullshitter, Bill."

"No," he said stubbornly. "You don't impose the mental limits and your physical limits— well, they are way down the road somewhere."

"Somewhere over the rainbow."

"I want you to go to Montreal a week early," he said without batting an eye.

"I am going a week early."

"A week earlier still. There are too many distractions around here. You said that your friends would be in Europe for a month."

"Yes, they're leaving this week."

"So, their apartment will be available to you?"

"Yes."

"I have it arrange.... "

"What will I tell Pop," Kay interrupted.

"Tell him that you need the other week. Tell him that I said so. Maybe, when the Games are over—when you are resting your legs—you can work some more time. You won't be staying there much longer anyway."

"He's already mad that I'm taking the week."

120

Bill shrugged off the objection.

"I will talk to him," he said, "man to man."

"Man to man."

"I have already spoken to Leon—my friend with the sleep capsule," Bill continued. "You will take your meals with him. He's a runner too. He knows what you need."

"No, no." Kay shook her head vigorously. "That's a hell of an imposition."

"It's no imposition. He has a housekeeper. He has plenty of time to spare. He has agreed to help with the workouts too."

Kay sighed. "A man who has a housekeeper and plenty of time to spare. I didn't know you had rich friends."

"He's not so rich. He has what he needs."

"How do you know he isn't after my body?"

"He is not after your body," Bill said calmly. "He is very interested in running. He does under 2:35 in the marathon. He jumped at the chance to work with you."

"Terrific. Does he do laundry?"

"He will arrange anything you need," Bill said, taking the question seriously. "He is expecting you on Monday. I told him that you would arrive in Montreal in the late afternoon."

"Did you buy my tickets too?"

Louise reappeared at that moment with a half-dozen donuts and three cups of coffee. "That line-up is ridiculous," she said as she put the tray down. "Did I miss anything?"

Kay shook her head. "No," she said, "nothing at all."

Chapter 16

Kay had just returned from her morning run when she heard the knock at the door. She assumed that the caller was the paperboy and felt inclined to ignore him. She knew that if she didn't pay him he would stop delivery and she did need her daily fix of sports news. Worse, he might send his mother to collect. She dug $2.40 out of the jar on the desk and went to the door.

The caller wasn't the paperboy after all. It was Esther, looking fresh and crisp in a white shirt and khaki shorts. "I hope I didn't disturb anything." Her eyes swept over the shorts and damp singlet. "You look as though you've been working."

"Just a brisk eight-mile run." Kay put the money back on the desk. "I thought you were the paperboy."

"I haven't been a paperboy in years." Esther leaned against the door frame expectantly. "Tab asked me to drop by to pick up some notes."

"Help yourself." Kay gestured toward the bedroom. "She has two closets full of them."

"She said they would be in a blue binder on the bedside table." Esther let herself in, finally, and closed the door.

Kay, who had recovered from her surprise by now, realized that she was being rude. "Sit down," she said, motioning toward a chair. "I'll see if I can find them."

The notes were on the bedside table, just as Tab had said.

Kay picked up the notebook and returned to the living room.

Esther was not in the living room. She was in the kitchen, helping herself to a cup of coffee. "I'm inviting myself to coffee," she said as she sat down at the kitchen table. "I have a few minutes to kill and the aroma of your coffee was irresistible."

"Thanks." Kay poured herself a cup of coffee and sat down opposite Esther. "It's my only vice."

Caesar circled Esther's chair warily. She tried to pat him but he moved away and jumped up into Kay's lap.

"Cats are strange animals," said Esther, unperturbed. "They do their best to avoid people who like them."

"I guess that's right," said Kay as Caesar rubbed against her fondly, "because I hate him and he won't leave me alone." In spite of her words she made no effort to put Caesar down. His obvious affection gave her a feeling of superiority.

"Do you prefer dogs?"

"No."

"I take it then that you don't care for animals."

Kay shrugged. "I like them fine," she said, "as long as they're outdoors catching mice, posing for Robert Bateman paintings or whatever it is they do."

Esther smiled and her eyes danced, the way Kay remembered them from their previous encounter. "Has anyone ever told you that you're a very funny woman?"

"I've been called a lot of things," Kay said sourly. "Funny has never been one of them."

"Don't you like to be thought of as funny?"

"I don't know." Kay looked into her coffee for a long moment. "No," she said finally, "I don't think so. We long-distance runners are a serious lot. We're running in memory of a man who dropped dead at the finish line after all. You know, Pheidippides. Rejoice, we are victorious and all that."

Esther merely smiled. "Tab tells me that you devote practi

123

cally every waking moment to some aspect of your sport. Running must be a serious business."

"It's my job," Kay said tersely, "except I don't get paid for it —at least not now. Someday, maybe, I'll get paid."

"I imagine that you would run even if you had no expectation of being paid—ever."

"Sure. Why not? I like it."

"Who does it benefit?"

"What?" Kay stared at Esther, taken aback by the sudden cross-examination.

"Most work benefits other people," Esther continued patiently. "That's why work has value. Who does your work benefit?"

"It benefits me," Kay said stoutly. "It benefits my fans. It benefits the little guy over on Dundas who sews my shoes together at $200 a shot."

"I suppose that's a start," said Esther, unimpressed. "I've always been curious about how athletes rationalize their existence," she continued. "What do sports contribute to the human condition?" Kay looked a little stormy and she hastened to add. "Tell me. I'd like to know."

Kay said grudgingly, "They make life tolerable for a lot of bored little people who work on assembly lines."

"Does running make life tolerable for you?"

"Very."

"What would you do without it?"

"I don't know." Kay shrugged. "I'd probably devote myself to some other magnificent endeavour. Maybe I'd go to Africa— you know, like Albert Schweitzer—open a clinic, be worshipped by the natives."

"Really?"

"No, I'm not that altruistic."

Esther did not respond, but continued to watch her keenly over folded arms.

"Look," Kay went on, "I'm an athlete. If I didn't run, I'd throw a javelin. If I didn't throw a javelin, I'd cycle. If sports weren't invented, I'd invent them. I'd do something great."

Esther was nodding. "I agree. You would be a star in whatever endeavour you chose. We—Tab and I and the others—agree that you have unusual potential for leadership."

"I'm flattered," Kay said dryly.

"If you were to join us. . . ."

"If."

"We would have to work with you, of course. We would have to modify some of your ways of thinking about. . . ."

"Indoctrinate me."

"Teach you the language, modify. . . ."

"I know most of the language," Kay interrupted airily. "Tab's been spouting it for years, after all."

"Modify certain attitudes."

"Such as?"

"Your very male attitude toward women."

"I beg your pardon?"

"It's obvious," Esther said calmly. "Look at your relationship with Tab. The distribution of labour alone is appalling. You do the macho—sports number. Tab does the housework, the laundry and—in her spare time—studies for her doctorate and lectures at the university."

"Tab doesn't like the way I do the housework," Kay said lamely.

"Do you know what Tab does at the university?"

"She does research. Sometimes she teaches."

"That's rather vague."

"She doesn't talk about it," Kay said abruptly.

"Perhaps you don't pay attention. Her Ph.D. thesis is considered to be brilliant, her field work remarkable. She would have been granted a Ph.D. long ago if her advisor wasn't such

125

a chauvinist. She's had to do twice as much work as would a male candidate working on a 'proper' subject. Did you know that?"

"No, I didn't."

"But she knows everything about your work. She knows your marathon and 10K times to the tenth of a second. She knows your training schedule like the back of her hand. She knows your past, your present and your dreams for the future."

"Tab likes sports," Kay said defensively. "At least, she used to like sports."

"She knows," Esther said pointedly, "because she listens. She listens to you, she nurtures your career, she attends to your every need."

"Tab likes to look after people."

"She has developed the nurturing role at the expense of self-actualization," Esther continued. "You encourage her to be nurturing by pretending to be totally dependent."

"Totally dependent!" Kay snorted. "Me, dependent!"

"Oh, Tab sees you as being thoroughly competent in dealing with the important aspects of your life," Esther said mildly. "You're the kingpin, the big star. And she's the adoring fan. At home, however—at least this is Tab's perception—she rules the roost. She views you as being incapable of preparing a meal or finding a clean pair of socks. In typical male fashion, you humour her. You joke about her being the boss, joke about how helpless you are, let the little woman think she's in control. In fact," she concluded, "you eschew housework because it's women's work. Running is men's work."

"That's bullshit," Kay said hotly. "I don't care if Tab does the housework or not. Hell, I could put starch in my running shorts—if I wanted starch in my running shorts. I could darn my own socks if I wanted to. I throw them away. Have you ever

126

tried to run in darned athletic socks? Do you think I need my salads fixed with the radishes cut up like little roses? Do you think I care whether or not she bleaches the house every second day? I'm hardly here long enough to enjoy it. Do you think I expect her to do all that shit?"

Kay paused and looked at Esther but, getting only a noncommittal gaze, continued. "The woman gets off on doing things like that. She's obsessive. I swear, she puts parsley in the cat's food. Last Christmas, she put a sprig of holly in his slop and almost poisoned him. I ask you, who needs that?"

"She invites friends to dinner and plans the entire event," Esther continued, unperturbed. "She remembers important occasions and buys gifts for mutual friends. She signs your name to the cards. She chooses your mother's birthday cards."

"Did she tell you all of that?"

"She didn't have to. I guessed. Such practices are standard in heterosexual relationships."

"She thinks I have lousy taste," Kay said lamely.

"And you take her to bed," Esther concluded, "because she has a great body."

"I suppose you guessed that too."

"Yes."

"It's none of your business."

"Let me rephrase my comment," Esther said briskly. "Have you ever wanted to go to bed with a woman who didn't have a great body? Have you ever wanted to go to bed with a woman because you appreciated her mind?"

"Sure. I've had the hots for Margaret Thatcher for years."

"Seriously?"

"Seriously?" Kay shrugged. "No," she confessed, "I've never wanted to go to bed with a woman who didn't have a great body. I love great bodies. I spend all my spare time, standing around on street corners, mentally undressing women."

127

There was a long pause, during which Esther studied Kay thoughtfully. "I believe that," she said finally. "You've been mentally undressing me since I walked in the door this morning." She picked up her coffee cup, balancing it delicately between her fingers. Her eyes were liquid with laughter. "What do you think of that, Kay Strachan?"

"I think that you're as arrogant as hell!"

"Do you want to go to bed with me?"

"No."

"Why not? I want to go to bed with you."

"Because you're Tab's lover." Kay looked at Esther in disbelief. "Because I'm Tab's best friend. I can't believe this!"

Esther nodded knowingly. "I know," she said. "You'd like to make love to me but I'm your best friend's girl. A man doesn't mess with his best friend's girl. That would constitute a violation of property rights."

Kay looked at Esther fiercely. "Does Tab believe all this crap?"

"Tab believes in open relationships."

"That's just a lot of stuff she spouts," Kay said stubbornly. "She's going through a phase. She's still waiting for her princess to come. I think she figures she's found her— if you know what I mean."

"Tab and I have an understanding."

"Sure you have an understanding—until the first night you don't come home."

"Tab can deal with that. She's a sophisticated woman."

"Sophistication can be painful."

"Tab's involved in a process of growth. That can be painful."

"I think I'd rather not grow then. I think I'd rather just hang around the locker room, looking and enjoying my own dirty thoughts. Nobody gets hurt that way. It's even fun." Kay slumped back in her chair, subdued. "I won't mention any of

128

this to Tab," she said.

"It doesn't matter."

"I think it does." Kay sat silently for a moment, staring at the tablecloth. "I imagine that Tab will be wanting her notes," she said finally.

"I imagine so." Esther sighed then gathered up the blue binder with a perky little shrug. "Well," she said, "thanks for the coffee and the conversation. It was very stimulating."

"Sure." Kay got up reluctantly and accompanied Esther to the door.

"I expect that we'll see one another in the not-too-distant future," Esther said.

"I expect so." Kay's eyes fell on the stack of mail on the telephone table. She scooped up the envelopes and handed them to Esther. "Why don't you take this stuff with you?" she said. "Just in case Tab doesn't come home for a few days."

"Of course." Esther tucked the envelopes inside the blue binder. She stood for a moment, looking at Kay solemnly. Then she was smiling again. She leaned forward and gave Kay a quick kiss, resting one hand lightly on her shoulder. "I hope you'll give some thought to what we've discussed."

"Sure." Kay tried to appear unmoved as Esther's hand lingered on her shoulder. She folded her arms to emphasize her indifference. It wasn't easy. Esther's blouse billowed as she leaned forward. Esther wasn't wearing a bra.

"Good bye."

Esther gave Kay's shoulder a final pat, then turned and strode out the door in one motion.

Kay waited until Esther disappeared around the landing then shut the door, shaking her head. The retreating footsteps seemed inappropriately cheerful.

She went to the bathroom and turned on the shower. She undressed quickly, tossing her clothes in the general direction

129

of the laundry hampers. Caesar followed her into the bathroom and positioned himself on the bathmat, paws folded into his chest.

Kay stepped into the shower, soaped her hair and body vigorously then rinsed quickly.

"That woman's immoral," she told Caesar as she stepped from the shower. "Gorgeous but immoral. It's a bad combination."

Caesar lifted his head, flickering an ear in protest as Kay sprayed him with a flourish of water droplets.

Kay positioned herself in front of the mirror and picked up the hairdryer. The high-pitched whine of the appliance caused Caesar to break out in a series of feeble squeaks. Kay looked at him disparagingly.

"What do you know about morality anyway?" she muttered. "If you weren't fixed, you'd be out ravaging half the neighbourhood."

She wafted the dryer over her head for a few minutes, staring pensively into the mirror. Then, her hair still wet, she turned the dryer off. She continued to stare into the mirror.

Caesar watched her gravely.

"Did you see that breast, Caesar?" she said softly. "I could have slipped my hand inside her shirt as easy as that." She flicked the plug of the hairdryer from the socket with a snap to illustrate the point. "Do you know how hard it was to resist?"

Caesar pulled himself up on his front legs and fixed her with a self-satisfied stare.

"What are you looking at?" Kay said crossly. "You'd cheat on your best friend without turning a whisker."

Caesar turned and left the room, swishing his tail peevishly. Kay folded the hairdryer and deposited it in the linen closet. As an afterthought, she picked up her clothes and the towel and deposited them neatly in the laundry basket.

Chapter 17

"Is that all you learned?" Kay asked as they drove back into Toronto late Saturday afternoon. "How to recognize and deal with common street drugs?"

"There are a lot of drugs out there."

"You' re telling me." Kay stretched out lazily in the passenger' s seat. "I'm a little disappointed, that's all. I thought you might have some juicy new information on domestic surveillance or cracking down on street runners."

"We should crack down on people who run in the streets," said Mary.

"I don't run in the streets. I use the sidewalks."

"Even in winter? I'm sure I've seen you running in the streets in winter."

"OK," Kay shrugged, "in the winter I very occasionally run in the streets."

"That's dangerous."

"I run facing the traffic. I wear gobs of reflective tape."

Mary brought the car to a halt at a red light."We scraped a runner off the street two years ago," she said. "He was wearing enough reflective tape to illuminate Yonge Street."

"I'm really very cautious," Kay protested. "Do you think I'd take a chance with this body?"

Mary was concentrating on the traffic.

"I hope not," she murmured. "It's a great body."

"Thank you." Kay wrapped her arms around her chest with a satisfied smile. It was a gesture that Tab would have called ultimately narcissistic.

The car moved deeper into the downtown area.

"What do you want to do now?" Mary asked.

"I don't know." Kay cast an eye over the heavy city traffic. "I have to shower and change," she said. "Then I suppose we could go out for dinner. I'll take you to Gus's."

Mary turned onto Church Street. "Come to my place," she said. "I'll make dinner."

"I was just kidding about Gus's. I'll take you to a nice place."

Mary brought the car to a halt in front of Kay's apartment building. "I'd like to make dinner for you."

"Are you sure?"

"Of course I'm sure." Mary removed the keys from the ignition and put them in her pocket. "I know a place about a mile from here that has the thickest, juiciest steaks and the best salad vegetables in Metro Toronto. I can do great things with steak and salad."

Kay acquiesced with a smile. "Sounds terrific," she said. She got out of the car and started up the steps to the apartment. She paused on the top step to wait for Mary who was putting coins into the parking metre. "Can't you get your tickets fixed?"

"I like to reserve that privilege for something worthwhile— like a twenty-dollar ticket for parking on Carleton overnight."

"Good. I'd hate to think you were that pure."

They walked up the steps to the apartment. Kay put the key into the lock, pausing rather apprehensively before opening the door. "I'm afraid the place is a bit of a mess," she said apologetically. "I didn't have time to clean up before I left this morning."

She pushed open the door and stopped dead in her tracks, a

look of surprise crossing her face.

"What's the matter?"

"Tab must have been here." Kay entered the apartment, scanning the living room slowly. "Either that or the White Tornado just whipped through."

There was a note on the refrigerator.

> *Kay,*
>
> *I fed Caesar. Kay, the place was a rat's nest. How can you stand it?*
>
> *P.S. I threw out your red singlet. I found it in the laundry basket, mildewed almost beyond recognition.*
>
> *P.S. I took your blue sweater to the dry cleaners. It looked as if it had been slept in for a week.*

Kay handed the note to Mary, shaking her head.

"Did you sleep in your blue sweater?"

"No, but I think Caesar did." Kay shrugged. "I was going to wash it," she said, "but I was afraid that the cat hair would clog the sewers from here to Whitby."

"There are some cups in the sink." Mary looked about the kitchen hesitantly. "Maybe I could wash them while you have your shower."

"Don't worry about them. They're probably getting their weekly dose of Javex." Kay leaned over the sink, sniffing cautiously. "Yup, that's Javex."

Kay filled the tea kettle and put it on the stove. "Relax. Make yourself a cup of tea. I'll be ready in a few minutes."

She collected fresh clothing from the bedroom and stepped into the bathroom, closing the door behind her. Like the rest of the apartment, the bathroom was in a state of pristine splendour. Tab had gone so far as to apply fresh, new labels to the laundry hampers. Kay stepped into the shower, feeling a stab of remorse as the first water droplets tainted the shiny fix-

133

tures. Her remorse was deepened by the knowledge that, if Tab returned in an hour and found her housekeeping efforts reduced to naught, she wouldn't give the disorder a second thought. She might even expect it.

That thought made Kay feel a little lonely. Then she remembered that Mary was waiting for her in the kitchen.

* * *

Mary's apartment was a shock to Kay. She had visualized a cozy nest with lots of overstuffed chairs and pictures of furry little animals lining the walls. Instead, the apartment seemed sterile—functional and practically devoid of personal touches.

Over dinner, she asked Mary how long she had lived there.

Mary's response made it apparent that she had read her thoughts. "Almost a year," she admitted. "I suppose I should do something with the place. I took it as a sublet. I never meant it to be permanent. Then, by the time it appeared that it would be at least semipermanent, I was used to it the way it was."

Kay shrugged. "That's the way I felt about my room in residence. Everybody else had stuffed toys, pictures of their grandmothers and the like. My room looked like a cell by comparison. I'd still live that way if it weren't for Tab. She loves having doilies all over the place and pictures on the walls."

"I guess you've known Tab for a long time."

"Yeah, we met on the track team in first year. Sometimes, though, I think I've known her forever."

"You'll miss her when she goes to North Borneo."

Kay shrugged, "I am kind of used to having her around. She'll probably send me little notes, telling me to use detergent when I do the laundry and the like. I'm sure she'll have her mother checking up on me. She could spend the rest of her life worrying that I might have lint on my shirt. To Tab, having lint on your shirt is worse than having a bat in your hair."

134

"Don't knock it. It's nice to have friends who care about you."

"Sometimes it's like going through life with your mother at your elbow." Kay sighed, then fell silent for a moment. "Dinner was great," she said finally. "You're right. You do terrific things with steak and salad."

"Thank you."

"I'll help you do the dishes," Kay added magnanimously.

"Do you want coffee first?"

"No, let's have coffee after. That way we won't have a greasy broiling pan staring us in the face."

Mary felt quite confident that Kay was not in the habit of fretting over greasy broiler pans. However, Kay made the offer so graciously that she was loathe to point this out. Instead, she acquiesced with a smile, led Kay into the kitchen and handed her a tea towel.

Kay knew they were going to make love but she was surprised when it happened. When the dishes were finished, Mary had simply taken the tea towel from her hand and led her into the bedroom. The coffee was forgotten. Mary brought it afterwards on a cafeteria-style tray with a bottle of liqueur.

"You said you were twenty-six before you slept with a woman," Kay ventured.

"Yes?"

"Why did you wait so long?"

"I was afraid—of what my family might think, afraid of being kicked out of the academy, afraid of losing my badge. When I finally got over being afraid, I was twenty-six."

"Who was she?" Kay asked hesitantly. "Your first lover?"

"Another cop," Mary said gently. "Constable Patricia York. Everybody called her Sergeant York, after the movie title."

"Did you call her Sergeant York?"

Mary shook her head. "No, I called her Pat. At first I called

135

her Yorkie but everybody picked up on that. So, I called her Pat."

"Were you together a long time?"

"Just over a year."

"What happened?"

Mary let her head drop back so that she was staring at the ceiling. "She never got over her first lover," she said simply. "Her name was Jan. She was killed in a car accident."

"Was she a cop too?"

Mary nodded and fell silent. Kay began to sip at her liqueur. Finally Mary continued. "I was so impatient," she said. "She was my first lover. I wanted everything to be perfect. I wanted her to see things through my eyes. Our first walk in the snow together. That sort of thing. But there was always this overlay. She'd done all those things before."

"That's tough."

"Before we were lovers, we would get together for a drink every now and then. She always wanted to talk about Jan. I thought, after we were together, she wouldn't need that anymore. I thought she would be able to put Jan away and forget about her."

"But she couldn't."

"No." Mary shook her head. "So, we decided to separate. It wasn't easy. We cared about each other. But she couldn't forget Jan and she knew it was making me unhappy."

"When did you split?"

"A year ago in September." Mary blinked at the ceiling, her eyes clouding. "If I'd been more understanding, we might still be together. But I felt as if I was competing against Jan all the time. She sounded so perfect. I panicked."

"Dead people are always perfect." Kay stared off into space. "It's the ones who are alive who are the pits. My ex-lover, for example. I can't think of a single good thing about her and I

136

can't think of a single good thing we ever did together. I slept with the damned woman for three years and I can't remember a good thing about that either."

"You're lucky. I think it's easier if you can leave the relationship feeling bitter. That way, you can cut the ties all at once and get on with your life."

"Do you ever see her?"

"No. She works in Scarborough. I haven't seen her since the day we moved out of the apartment." Mary paused, her lower lip trembling. "She helped me pack my things," she continued haltingly. "There were some things that we'd had together. She wanted me to take them. I wanted her to take them. Neither of us wanted them."

"What to do with the stuff you accumulate together," Kay said with a sigh. "When I arrived on Tab's doorstep, I didn't have a thing except my running gear and fifty-thousand copies of *Runners' World*. Tab went over to my place afterwards and picked up a few things she thought I might want—like my clothes and my toothbrush. A couple of days later a box appeared with my trophies. A few weeks later, two more boxes appeared. Bonnie was moving out of the apartment about that time and decided to send along the leftovers." Kay smiled ruefully. "Every time something else arrived, I would get furious all over again. By the time the last box arrived, I was so angry that I took it right down to the street and put it out with the garbage. Tab went down later and picked through the stuff. She didn't tell me this right away. She hid the stuff in a closet and brought it out gradually."

"Did you throw it out again?"

"No. Most of it was stuff Tab had given us—gifts to Bonnie and me as a couple. She explained that she had bought the stuff mainly with me in mind. That made me feel a little better about it."

"I put all the things I'd had with Pat in boxes and stored them in my parents' attic. It was three months before I was able to do that much. Putting those things away was almost as painful as the breakup itself."

"Well, I sure didn't feel that way about it," Kay said grimly. "I could have thrown everything in the garbage. Even my trophies. At that point, everything seemed tainted. Tab said I would have regretted turfing my trophies but I don't know."

"You were lucky to have a place to go. I spent the first week in a motel. It was nice of Tab to offer you a place to stay."

"She didn't." Kay folded her arms behind her head with a smile. "When I came hammering at her door, she was in the sack with a little cutie from the psych department. She yelled at me to wait on the landing. By the time she opened the door, I was in tears. She felt really sorry then. She sent the psych student home and made me a big batch of brownies. Food is Tab's solution to almost everything."

"Is Esther her lover?"

"Yes."

"For a long time?"

"No, just for a few months."

"Was there someone before Esther?"

"There were lots of women before Esther."

"No one special?"

"No." Kay shrugged. "Tab falls in love a lot. She likes to pretend that sex and love fill a perfectly functional role in her life —ideology, she would call it—but she falls in love a lot."

"Falling in and out of love all the time must be painful."

"Yeah," Kay acknowledged, "but Tab doesn't stay hurt very long. A lot of it is infatuation."

"What about Esther?"

"I don't know." Kay was silent for a moment."Well, maybe this time it's not infatuation," she conceded."She has lasted a lot longer than most of them."

"It's funny," Mary murmured. "Tab seems so straightforward, so practical. She seems like the sort of woman who would have settled into a permanent relationship a long time ago."

"It's an illusion." Kay wrinkled her brow into a frown. "Tab lives life like a page out of a storybook, one of those kids' books with the blue skies and the puffy white clouds. She's sort of a Mary Poppins—whipping around with a bunch of balloons in her hand, spreading joy and keeping everything tidy. She's too busy to settle into a permanent relationship."

"Maybe this time."

"Maybe."

Mary reached over and took Kay's hand. For a few minutes neither of them spoke.

"I'm glad you came here tonight," Mary said finally.

"I'm glad I came here too."

She wondered if Mary wanted to make love again but Mary seemed content just to hold her hand. She knew that Mary would be working a double shift the next day and there would be no time for love-making in the morning. She felt that she should make a gesture but she really didn't feel like it. She felt like talking instead.

She talked about herself—about her running past and about the Olympics and about her running future. She felt as if she had been talking for hours when, in fact, it was only minutes. Mary didn't say anything but Kay knew she was listening.

She knew the exact moment when Mary fell asleep. The grip on her hand relaxed and she started to breathe deeply and evenly.

Kay turned her head for a moment to watch her, then, with a sigh, fell asleep herself.

139

Chapter 18

When Kay woke the next morning, Mary was already dressed and strapping on her holster. "I didn't know if I should let you sleep or wake you and drive you home."

Kay stretched out with a huge yawn. "You don't have to drive me home. I'll run home."

"Are you sure?"

"Sure, I'm sure." Kay swung her legs over the side of the bed and stood up. "One of the great things about a wardrobe of perpetual sweats is that you're always ready to run."

"I'll get you some coffee."

Mary went into the kitchen and poured the coffee into a thick white mug.

Kay took it from her as she passed by on her way to the bathroom. "Thanks."

She paused to give Mary a little kiss as she took the mug.

Kay went into the bathroom, stopped at the sink to wash her hands and face.

Mary's voice floated to her from the kitchen. "I'll have to leave in a few minutes. There's cereal in the cupboard if you want something to eat."

"No thanks." Kay emerged from the bathroom, cup in hand. "I was planning on leaving with you." She went to the bedroom and collected her clothing.

Mary followed her into the room and sat on the bed as she

140

dressed. "I'm sorry I have to work today. Sunday morning is such a nice morning to relax and read the newspapers, have breakfast, whatever."

"Whatever?"

Mary smiled. "Whatever is what you do after you've had breakfast and read all the newspapers."

"I see."

"Maybe next weekend, before you go to Montreal."

"Damn." Kay flushed suddenly.

"What's the matter?"

"I won't be here next weekend." Kay bent hastily to tie her shoelaces. "I'm going to Montreal a week early. I forgot," she said lamely. "I meant to tell you."

"It's all right."

Kay paused for a moment, then shook her head. "No," she said, subdued, "I didn't forget. It's just that we were having such a good time yesterday. I didn't want to ruin it."

"Thank you."

"I don't think you should thank me. I should have let you know right away."

"Thank you for not wanting to ruin yesterday." Mary shrugged a little sadly. "I am sorry that you have to go to Montreal a week early and I'm sorry that I have to work today. But yesterday was good," she added softly. "Nothing can ruin it."

"I'll call you from Montreal," said Kay, relieved. "I thought a week down there would be enough but Bill doesn't think so. He thinks that the other girls—Debbie, Louise—are giving me nerves, agonizing about their preparations. He thinks that, with the women's marathon happening so early, I need the extra time to relax."

"I guess he's right."

"I guess so. He usually is." Kay shrugged. "He had it all lined up, even before he told me. He's got somebody to help with

141

my training, fix my meals.... "

"I'll think about you while I'm getting indigestion at Gus's."

"I'll think about you too."

There were a few moments of silence, then Kay knew it was time to go. She kissed Mary again before they left the apartment and gave her hand a squeeze just before she got into the car and drove away.

Kay didn't start to run immediately. She stood on the sidewalk in front of Mary's apartment and watched until the car was well out of sight.

* * *

Sunday was a rest day. Kay ran the five miles to the apartment at an easy pace, languidly counting out the steps in her head. It was a warm July morning, already too warm and too humid for the hour. The gas fumes rose into her nostrils as she ran. By the time she reached the apartment, she was glowing and—in spite of the humidity—quite refreshed.

She was fumbling with her key when the door opened. Tab stood framed in the doorway, looking rather weary.

"What in hell are you doing here?"

"I live here."

"I mean, at this hour?" Kay pulled off the sodden sweatshirt and threw it over the arm of the easy chair."I thought you were spending the night with Esther."

"I was." Tab went to the kitchen to fetch the teapot. She carried it into the living room and set it on the table beside the easy chair. She sat down in the chair, dropping the sweatshirt to the floor with an expression of distaste."I spent most of last night in the emergency department at the Wellesley," she said.

"Was Esther sick?"

"No." Tab sipped her tea with a sigh of appreciation."Debbie was out drinking with some friends last night. Someone

142

slammed her finger in a car door."

"Shit!"

"The index finger of her throwing hand was broken," Tab continued. "She's distraught."

"Shit!"

"She tried to call you but she couldn't find you. She tried to call Louise but she couldn't find Louise either. Finally, she located me at Esther's."

"What happened to the friends she was drinking with?"

"They did what they could. They took her to the emergency department. They tried to be helpful. She didn't want them. She wanted you."

"Damned!" Kay sat down on the sofa with a sigh.

"I told her that you would call her later today. I think she's sleeping now." Tab paused. "I hope she's sleeping now. They gave her enough sedation to floor a hippopotamus."

"And even that wasn't enough," Kay murmured.

"You should be shot for saying that, Kay."

"I should be shot." Kay shook her head. "Bill was right. He knew it was going to get squirrely around here."

"Bless Bill."

"Is it bad?" Kay remembered that she was supposed to be thirsty. She went into the kitchen and poured a glass of apple juice.

"It was a crushing injury. It is not a clean break, Kay." Tab followed her with her eyes as she returned to the sofa. "It isn't something that the trainers can perform miracles on before the Games."

"Hell." Kay sat down with a thump. "She was good, you know. She didn't look at all shabby beside the East Europeans."

"She's distraught."

"Yeah, I would be too." Kay stared at the glass in her hand. "But she's only twenty-four. She's got a couple of Games ahead of her. These throwers have longevity."

"Tell her that when you call."

"I will."

"Better still, why don't you go to see her this afternoon?"

"Christ, Tab," Kay said irritably, "she'll want me to hug her and everything. Remember what she was like when she pulled her back muscle?"

"It won't kill you to hug her, Kay."

"What was she doing anyway—out in a bar, two weeks before the Olympics, getting so sloppy that she got her finger caught in a car door?"

"She was with a new woman," Tab explained patiently. "You know how nervous she gets with a new woman."

"Damn!"

"I'll go with you."

Kay shook her head in resignation. "OK, I'll go," she said. "But, you've got to go in first. Maybe you can dissipate some of the hugs before I get to the door."

"Agreed." Tab stood up and headed for the kitchen. "Have you had breakfast?"

"No."

"I'll make you some French toast."

"That sounds great." Kay stretched out on the sofa with a sigh. She wasn't keen on visiting Debbie but visiting Debbie would please Tab and, hence, save her from one of Tab's lectures. Besides, today she could afford to be agreeable. Tomorrow, she would be away from it all.

* * *

"I think we had her cheered up by the time we left," Kay said to Tab as they drove away from Debbie's apartment that evening.

"Hm." A light rain was falling and Tab stared earnestly

through the wiper blades. "I think you could have said something a little more uplifting than life is shitty," she said seriously. "Later in life, people like to remember what friends said in times of crisis."

"I think she liked it. Besides, remember what you said about expressing my true self?"

"I remember." The rain was getting heavier and Tab started to blink.

"I wish you'd wear your glasses when you drive."

"I am." Tab downshifted abruptly. "I'm wearing contacts."

"Really." Kay looked at Tab in surprise. "Well, when did this happen?"

"A couple of weeks ago. The doctor said that I would get a more accurate correction with contacts."

"That's too bad." Kay shrugged. "I liked your glasses. I thought they made you look mature, more in keeping with your station in life."

"I was tired of them."

"I'll bet Esther didn't like them." Kay started to laugh. "I'll bet she thought that they hid those baby-blue eyes."

"She thought that contacts would give me a more accurate correction," Tab said evenly.

"She didn't care how they looked."

"No." Tab waited patiently for the intersection to clear. "She never raised the issue."

"Silly woman." Kay started to say something on that topic then suddenly remembered that she didn't want to talk about Esther. For the next block, she said nothing. "Do you remember when we were freshmen on the track team?" she said finally. "When you still believed in sports?"

"Believed in sports somewhat," Tab interrupted.

"Whatever." Kay waved the comment aside impatiently. "We used to talk about going to the Olympics, waving our Canadian flags, marching in the parade in whatever God-awful outfit they'd chosen for us."

"I remember."

"And everyone would be cheering and they'd be handing out the gold medals as if they were going out of style. The TV announcer would be screaming and everybody back home would be having a party. There would be pictures of us on the front page of The Globe and stories inside about how the kid from Welland had made us all proud to be Canadians."

"Yes."

"Then when I got to the Pan Am Games it was such a shock." Kay shook her head. "You know, I was sure I was going to win a medal. After all, I was the third best middle-distance runner in the country. I was shocked when I saw how fast and how good they were. I felt as if I was running in slow motion. And it was all over so fast. Our best runner—the girl who beat me every Saturday—didn't make it out of the semifinal heat. And I thought I was going to win a medal."

"You were always very confident, Kay. You always thought you would win."

"Yeah." Kay stretched out with a smile. "Well, this time I'm going to. I'm going to stand up there on that podium and they're going to hand me the flowers and put the gold medal around my neck. They'll be screaming all the way to Inuvik."

"It sounds like a coronation."

There was a silence then the smile faded. "I wish you were with me on this, Tab."

"I was never good enough to go to the Olympics, Kay. I was strictly all-Ontario."

"I don't mean that. I mean with me for the race. Remember how you used to come along to the meets? We'd cheer for Louise. Then you and Louise would cheer for me. And later, when I was doing 10K's and marathons, you and Louise and

146

Debbie would come down and throw water on me. Then you'd all jump into the car and move along to the next check-point, throw some more water, wave a few banners. Then, afterwards, we'd all get together for a beer. You used to be like a kid on Christmas Eve before those races. You'd have me so psyched up, I'd be running on air."

"I thought Bill was sending you to Montreal early to save you from that sort of thing."

"I know." Kay emitted a long audible sigh. "He doesn't like me living on nerves for two weeks before a race. That's why he got me out of town before Helsinki too. But what the hell, I loved it."

"I loved it too." Tab rolled the window down a couple of inches and Kay focussed on the intensified sound of the rain. "I loved it when it was happening. You were such an underdog in those days, Kay. You were running against all those classy runners with the company logos plastered all over their singlets, with the shiny ads in all the magazines."

"I guess I'm not an underdog anymore, huh?"

"No." Tab shook her head. "And Louise and I haven't followed you around, throwing water on you for at least two years."

"I guess not." Kay shrugged. "But it's nice to think about it. It doesn't seem that long ago."

"If I thought you needed it, I'd take a banner to Montreal, throw water on you, whatever—in spite of my principles. But you don't need it. You are a prohibitive favourite, according to *The Star* this morning, according to everyone who knows anything about running."

"A prohibitive favourite," Kay murmured. "Are these guys trying to take all the fun out of the race? Don't they know how unpredictable the marathon can be?"

"You've proven yourself, over and over again," said Tab,

quoting *The Star* again, "against the toughest competition. To fail is not an expression in your vocabulary."

"I see."

"I want you to win, Kay."

"Thanks a lot."

"Because you're my friend, because I know what you've invested, because I doubt if any of your competitors is committed to anything more altruistic than herself."

"Thanks again. You're giving me a terrific send-off."

"I'd be disappointed if you didn't win."

"You're doing better."

"I'd be very disappointed if you didn't win."

"I guess I can live with that."

Tab pulled the car to a stop as the amber light changed to red. "Did you stay with Mary last night?" she asked casually.

"What makes you think that I did?"

"Am I to assume that you've started to make your bed at six o'clock in the morning?"

"I spent the night with Mary."

"How did it go?"

"Good, it was very good."

"I'm glad." Tab changed gears as the light turned green. "Will she be going to Montreal?"

"She can't take time off work."

"In that case, why don't you invite her to Montreal after the Games? She might be able to arrange time off in a couple of weeks. Nicole and Steacy will be away for a month. You could spend some time together, enjoy the city."

"I lied." Kay stared into her lap. "I don't know if she can get time off or not. I didn't ask her."

"Kay!"

"I didn't think that far ahead," Kay said defensively. "I'm going to be really busy for the next few days. What am I supposed to do? Invite her to Montreal so she can spend the whole day, watching me work out?"

Tab looked at Kay, then shook her head. "Well," she conceded, "perhaps you're right."

"We did have a good time yesterday. After the workout, we drove around Kleinburg for hours, just talking. She's very easy to talk to, very easy to be with."

"And she didn't make you feel guilty?"

"About what?"

"About not inviting her to Montreal."

"She didn't have to. You're doing it for her."

"I think she's too easy on you." Tab brought the car to a halt in front of the apartment building. "You slept with the woman. Now, you're tripping off to Montreal. You didn't invite her and I doubt if you offered to telephone."

"Well, you're wrong about that, Tab." Kay had her hand on the door handle. "You've got me mad now, and I'll bet you're going to run off to Esther and leave me to get an ulcer."

"No." Tab removed the keys from the ignition. "I'm not running off to Esther. I told her that I had to get up early to see you off at the train."

"Really?"

"Really. Also, I told Debbie that we would pick her up. She wants to see you off at the train too."

"That's very nice of Debbie."

"Yes. When she was hugging me good bye tonight—in spite of her pain—she made me promise not to forget to pick her up tomorrow morning."

They got out of the car. Tab locked the doors while Kay waited for her on the sidewalk. "She's very fond of you, Kay. You should be touched."

"She has the hots for me."

"I know. *Almost* every woman in North America has the

149

hots for you."

"Now you're talking."

Kay followed Tab up the apartment steps and waited patiently as Tab searched for her keys. "Sleep with me tonight."

"Every woman in North America has the hots for you."

"I mean, sleep with me."

"I'm tired. I need a good night's sleep. I seldom get that when I share my bed with you."

"I'll sleep on the couch then."

"Good." Tab went directly to the bathroom and began to brush her teeth. When she came out of the bathroom, Kay had a sleeping bag spread out on the couch and was preparing to climb into it. "It's cozier than my bed," she explained.

Tab undressed, got into bed and fell into a deep sleep immediately. She was awakened within minutes. Kay was shaking her elbow vigorously.

"I'm not comfortable."

"Jesus Christ!"

"I promise to be quiet." Kay squeezed into the bed beside her.

"I was asleep, Kay."

"I thought you just had your eyes closed."

"Is that why you tried to break my arm?" Tab suddenly sat bolt upright and turned on the bedside lamp. "Damn!"

"What's the matter?"

"I forgot to take my contacts out." Tab got out of bed and went into the bathroom.

Kay was waiting for her, propped up on one elbow when she returned. "I guess I saved your eyes, huh?"

"Go to sleep." Tab crawled back into bed and switched off the light.

There was a long silence. Tab glanced at Kay suspiciously.

"Did you remember to reserve your train ticket?"

"Bill did it for me."

"I should have known."

"What do you mean, you should have known? Does Wayne Gretsky make his own travel arrangements? Does Walter Payton go down and stand in line for tickets? What's the matter with Bill getting my tickets?"

Tab had turned over onto her side. Kay leaned over so that she was whispering into her ear. "Is it because I'm a woman, Tab? Are you showing some deep, unconscious prejudice against your own kind? Are we witnessing some symptom of your insecurity about the status of women in our society?"

"It's because you enjoy it so damned much." Tab turned to Kay, eyes ablaze, then immediately fell back to her pillow. "Go to sleep, Kay."

"I love it when you swear." Kay waited for a reply but Tab was resolute, so she lay back, chuckling to herself.

Then she thought about Mary and her thoughts sobered her instantly.

Chapter 19

Bill was at Union Station when they arrived the next morning. He told Kay that he had wanted to surprise her.

The first-class tickets were also a surprise.

"I couldn't have you going to the Games in the coach car," he told her. "When I thought more about it, I guessed that I should have sent you on the plane. But it was too late then and I know that you don't like to fly that much."

"I hate flying, Bill."

"So, the club car will be great. You can relax and do what you want."

"You're a sweetheart, Bill."

They had breakfast together while they waited for the train. Debbie had thrown on a baggy sweatsuit. Tab's hair was still rumpled from sleep.

Bill, however, looked as pristine as always. "I phoned Leon last night and confirmed all of the details." He reached into the inside pocket of his suit jacket and took out a manila envelope. "Just in case, I wrote everything down. Give this to Leon when he meets you." He handed the envelope to Kay.

"Can I read it?"

"No, it's for Leon."

"What's in it? A year's supply of dirty jokes?"

"No, there are no jokes. It's your schedule, other things about you."

"My, my! Now I'll have to read it."

"Just give it to Leon."

"Yes, sir."

"I will be phoning you in a couple of days."

"Super."

The public address system announced the arrival of Kay's train—first in French, then in English. Bill paid for breakfast then escorted Kay solemnly to the platform.

"I want you to enjoy yourself," he said as they lingered at the gate.

"I will." She knew that he was trying to express affection so she gave him a little pat on the shoulder and a smile. He coughed fussily.

Tab gave Kay a rather grumpy hug. She hadn't slept well. Debbie hugged her too and pressed a Mother Nature is a Lesbian button into her hand. Kay held it in her hand until she boarded the train then tossed it quickly into her equipment bag.

* * *

The club car was comfortable. Too comfortable. After Kay got over her excitement about being in it, she fell asleep and didn't wake up until Dorval.

As the train chugged into Montreal, she had a few minutes to reflect upon the previous evening.

It had been childish to wake Tab but she was miffed at Tab's indifference, particularly since she had been so cooperative in commiserating with Debbie. She thought about Tab and about Debbie and felt guilty. Then she thought, What the hell, and then she said the words out loud. The club car was so quiet that everyone heard her and several people turned to stare at her.

* * *

The man who met her at Central Station was Bill's age. He was wearing a rumpled tweed jacket over a Roman collar. He recognized her at once and held out his hand.

153

"Leon Dupre."

Kay gulped. "Bill didn't tell me you were a priest."

"He knew that you wouldn't come if you knew that." Leon Dupre took her luggage and pointed her in the direction of the exit. "My car is in the parking lot."

Kay waited while the priest stowed her luggage in the trunk of the battered blue sedan.

"The car's a clunker," Leon said cheerfully as he slid behind the wheel. "The parishioners wanted to buy me a new one. I talked them into a sleep tank instead."

"For your meditations?"

"Sure. I finagled a home fitness center as well. Do you do Nautilus?"

"Free weights."

"I have those too. I've set up a gym in the basement of the rectory."

"Sounds great."

"Fitness is also a form of prayer."

"Of course."

"The place you're staying is very close to us," Leon added. "That's a happy coincidence." He pulled the car to a stop at a red light. "By the way, Bill said that you would have a letter for me."

Kay pulled the manila envelope from her pocket and handed it to him."Sorry, it's a bit crumpled. I slept on it."

Leon opened the envelope and scanned the pages briefly. "No workout today," he announced. "You're to have dinner at the rectory and I will introduce you to the tank."

"Sounds fine."

"I will drop you off at your accommodations then. At five o'clock I will pick you up for dinner." He shrugged apologetically. "The housekeeper likes everything cleared away early. She has television shows that she has to see."

"I guess she won't be joining us for our workout then."

"Ha, you have a sense of humour. That's good. Bill said that you were very serious."

"A lot of people think I'm funny lately."

"Of course, Bill has no sense of humour so he wouldn't know. I've always told him that that was why his marriage failed. He couldn't laugh at anything."

"How long have you known Bill?"

Leon snorted amiably. "Hell, we were kids together in Shawinigan Falls. We ran cross-country together in high school and again in university. Sure," he continued, shaking his head nostalgically, "I have know Bill since he was, maybe, eight years old, since we were playing street hockey. He was just a scrawny little kid and always had a bloody nose. The big boys used to beat him up."

"He said he always wanted to play hockey."

"Sure, all French-Canadian boys of our generation wanted to play hockey. It was our heritage. But Bill was no good at it. He wanted to run the marathon too. That was his big dream."

"But he was no good at that either."

"No, he was not so good at that either. Well," Leon shrugged, "he was better than myself but he was not as good as he wanted to be."

"I think that's a shame."

"Perhaps so. But, he became a real student of the marathon. Some people think it is so simple, you know. You just go out there and run a long way, they think. But, of course, as you know and as I know it's really very complex. Bill devotes himself to every detail. He feels that there is always so much more to learn. I admire that in him—always wanting to be so good at something and never being satisfied." Leon made a left-hand turn with carefree disregard for the yellow light. "I was surprised when he said that he was sending you to me—and honoured. I never thought that I would take part in coaching an Olympian."

"We're even. I never thought that I'd ever be coached by a priest."

"Actually I shouldn't say that I'm coaching," Leon went on. He paused, tapping the envelope in his pocket. "These don't leave much room for initiative. Still, it is a privilege."

"Thank you."

Leon started to talk about the marathon route. Kay pretended to listen but her mind kept drifting. She knew the Olympic route by heart. Leon had made it to the twenty-mile mark by the time they pulled up in front of the apartment.

"Rest," he told her. "I'll be back at five."

* * *

She didn't think that she would sleep but, when Leon rang the doorbell at five, she was dozing in front of the television set.

" This is it." Leon stopped in front of a long, egg-shaped object in one corner of the exercise room.

"It looks like a coffin."

"It's very comfortable."

"Couldn't they have at least put a window in the lid?"

"That would defeat the purpose. Are you claustrophobic?"

"No."

"Then you have nothing to worry about."

"How do I breathe?"

"There are air holes."

"I'm going to feel like a package from the pet store."

"You will enjoy it. Once you get in it, you will not want to get out."

"How long do I stay in it?"

"Forty-five minutes. Perhaps an hour." Leon reached over and flipped open the lid. "As you can see," he said, "the solution is only ten inches deep. The water is made perfectly buoyant by the addition of large quantities of Epsom's salts."

"What if I don't want to stay in for forty-five minutes?" Kay worried.

"Then you will open the lid and get out."

"Good."

"You will find it very comfortable," Leon repeated. "Once you realize that you are floating, you will forget that you are in water at all. You will think that you are on a cloud." Leon paused, clearing his throat slightly. "To get full advantage of the tank, I recommend that you wear a bathing suit that is fully formfitting."

"Formfitting?"

"Yes, loose fabric is a distraction. Don't worry," he added hastily, "you will have complete privacy." He took Bill's instructions from his pocket and reviewed them once again. "You will use the tank every day," he said, "the free weights every other day as you have been doing all along. Tomorrow morning you will do three easy miles. I have selected a pleasant route for you. It is one I run myself."

"Hills?"

"No hills. Bill specifies no hills. The marathon course is almost flat. The hills will not give you even a psychological advantage. You have your strength base. In the afternoon, you will do hard miles—three of them—just a little faster than race pace. The hard miles will be done on the marathon course."

"On the course?"

"Yes." Leon was still perusing the notes. "I will drive you to a different section of the course each day. In the race, you will remember each section and you will remember that you covered the distance very quickly. You will run each mile at 5:00 pace. In the race—at a slower pace—it will seem easy."

"What else?"

157

"A warm-down walk of a mile after the hard run," Leon continued. "Then rest, then dinner, then the tank."

"What about the next day?"

"The same. Your total mileage is not to exceed the thirty-six miles specified. Sunday is a rest day as usual—a day to relax. Bill suggests that I take you to an Expos game."

"You call that relaxing?"

"Bryn Smith is scheduled to pitch."

"Don't you have to work on Sunday? Do a mass? Preach a sermon?"

"I will be finished by game time." Bill glanced at his watch. "I have to go out this evening," he said, "so I will drive you home now. In the morning, Bill wants you to sleep in until eight at least. I will pick you up at nine for your workout. After, we will have breakfast."

"Good." Kay nodded slowly. "OK. Nine it is."

* * *

Bill telephoned shortly after she arrived back at the apartment.

"So, how did you and Leon get along?"

"Just fine, Bill."

"Good. Leon's a fine guy. How do you like your schedule?"

"It's great, Bill. It's like being on vacation."

"I hope I haven't neglected anything. I don't think so I reviewed it pretty carefully."

"You forgot to tell me what to think about in the tank."

"What?" he said surprised. "Why do I have to tell you that? Think about what suits you. Think about the great races you've done."

"Maybe I'll think about you when you were a little kid," she said mischievously, "running around playing hockey in your Canadiens sweater and your bow tie."

"Think about your races, Kay."

158

"Right, Coach."

"Louise asked me to say hello."

"Thanks. Say hello to her too."

"She's a little nervous. I should send her to Montreal too. But I don't want you in Montreal together. Sometimes you're not good for each other."

"Is she telling you the story about the frog again?"

"No, she didn't say anything about that—at least not to me, not recently. Her times, today and yesterday, were not what they should be."

"Everybody has bad days, Bill."

"Yes, but for her it is psychologically damaging. I think she is into her peak pretty well. I don't want her to be dwelling on one or two sour workouts."

"So, I'll bet you lied to her and told her that her times were great."

"Of course I did. What else should I do? I expect that she will be back on track tomorrow."

"Either that or she's had the shortest peak in the history of track and field."

"I cannot believe that." Bill sighed audibly. "If so, I will lose the rest of my hair for sure."

"Poor Bill." Kay tried to sound sympathetic. "At least you don't have me to worry about."

"You I don't need to worry about," he said, refreshed. "All the hard work is done. Leon thought that you looked great."

"You've been talking to Leon already?"

"We spoke this afternoon."

"What did you think could happen in five hours? Did you think I'd make a mistake and get off the train in Cornwall?"

"Of course not. I wanted to make sure that the instructions were very clear to him. And, I wanted to make sure that the two of you would hit it off."

"We're practically bosom buddies."

"I thought so. But, just in case, I had to check—in the event that I would have to make alternate arrangements."

"Bill, I think you should run a hot bath, get into it, take two aspirins and go to sleep."

"Actually, I was thinking of pouring a scotch and watching the news. Sometimes it is refreshing to know that what goes on at the University of Toronto track is not the worst thing happening in the world."

"I'm sure it isn't."

"I'll say good night then and I will call you later in the week."

"Good night, Bill." Kay paused to see if he would hang up the receiver. "You're a real sweetheart for worrying about me. If you were here, I would kiss you."

"No, you wouldn't." He said this and hung up immediately.

* * *

Kay was in bed and half-asleep before she realized that she had forgotten to call Mary. She rolled out of bed and placed the call.

There was no answer. Kay dialed again in case she had dialed a wrong number.

Then she remembered that Mary was on duty until midnight and probably wouldn't arrive home until after one a.m.

Kay went back to bed, resolving to call Mary between workouts the next day.

Chapter 20

The workouts were going splendidly—the morning runs just sufficient to loosen and relax, the afternoon runs not so hard as to risk injury but difficult enough to ward off restlessness. The meals too had been carefully planned so that she was never hungry yet varied not a pound from her normal weight. Bill's plan was, in fact, total deceit producing the illusion of a full day's work with scarcely a third of the normal energy expenditure.

And waiting for her at the end of each day was the reward of an hour in the tank. The tank was warm and soothing and after the first two days she didn't worry about drowning at all. Leon respected her privacy but she knew that he was hovering near the door on the upper floor in the event of an emergency. After the third day, Leon too slipped to the back of her mind.

She called Mary on the fourth day, apologizing for her tardiness. Mary listened attentively and enjoyed her stories about training with Leon. Mary didn't make her feel guilty at all but Kay could feel Tab's eyes boring into the back of her head all the way from Toronto and felt guilty nonetheless.

In the tank, she concentrated very hard, conjuring up images of all her great races as Bill had suggested. The images gave eloquent testimony to the beautiful free-flowing stride, the effortless speed. They were magnificent and she told Leon about them. Leon was thrilled and questioned her about them in great detail. He ran with her during the morning workouts and asked about the tank images again between laboured breaths.

On Sunday, Leon took her to the Expos game. It was the final game of the current homestand and was played in Jarry Park, Olympic Stadium having been torn to rat shit for the Olympics. It was more fun to watch a game in Jarry Park, Leon told her. It was like the old days. Bryn Smith pitched a six-hitter but still lost. Leon left muttering about how the Expos still needed a third baseman who could hit in the clutch. The CTV announcer spotted her in the audience and the stadium crew flashed a big welcome to her on the scoreboard. Kay tried to smile and hoped that her friends back home wouldn't catch her hobnobbing with a priest.

By the seventh day Kay was tired of the running images. She pretended instead that she was in the middle of a vast, gently lapping ocean. There was nothing to be seen for miles except the odd friendly turtle. Sometimes the turtle carried a pot of tea on his back and sometimes he wore a red hat. Whatever his accoutrements, he was always sleepy-eyed and congenial.

When she got tired of the turtle, she conjured up a shallow, pale green lagoon sprinkled with soft brown sandbars. The water was buoyant and warm and wonderfully erotic against her skin.

And then she thought about Mary—about the nipples that seemed so pink against the soft white skin and the mound of hair, soft and silky like the hair on her head and just a little darker. Tab's hair was, in contrast, thick—she conjured up that image too—and much darker. Louise's was densely charcoal and carefully trimmed to accommodate her track shorts. Esther, Kay guessed, was the kind of woman who would have pubic hair to her knees, curly, luxurious, and glossy black.

162

Kay imagined making love to Esther and then to Mary and then to Tab. Each provided a pleasant bit of reverie.

She was forced to fabricate some running images for Leon. He listened politely but said that they weren't as good as the earlier accounts and suggested that she switch her meditations to a different subject.

Bill phoned and suggested that she imagine herself on the podium. That, he said, is what he would do. Instead, she went back to the lagoon and made love to all three women in the green water.

* * *

Five days before the race, Kay heard the news. She saw the story in the morning papers but it was after midnight before Tab called.

Tab didn't take time to say hello. "Have you heard?" she asked urgently.

"Heard what?"

"About Mary."

"Yes, I heard." Kay looked at the floor automatically to avoid the imagined gaze. "I read about it in The Star this morning."

"Kay," Tab said, bewildered, "why aren't you here?"

"I can't."

"What do you mean, you can't?"

"Because I'm training." Kay took a deep breath. "Because I'm racing in less than a week."

"I don't believe this, Kay." Kay could imagine the lines around Tab's mouth tightening. "The woman's lying in TGH with tubes coming out of her in every direction because a little delinquent thought she was after his cocaine and slipped a knife between her ribs."

"I called," Kay said lamely. "They—the nurse, people in her room—they said she was out of danger and would be OK."

"I think you should be here right now."

163

"I sent flowers."

"You sent flowers." Tab's tone was suddenly hard and flat.

"Yeah, I phoned Jean and asked her...."

"Oh," said Tab with sarcastic enlightenment, "the ones from The Girls at Pop's."

"I can't come," Kay persisted. "Mary will understand."

"I can't believe this, Kay. This is absolutely the most selfish, most despicable thing you have ever done." Tab paused to let her words sink in. "You have no intention of coming, do you?"

"No." The receiver in her hand felt suddenly icy. "Will you be down soon?" she ventured timidly.

There was a long pause then Tab slammed the receiver down.

Kay held the receiver in her hand for a moment, the noise still ringing in her ears. Finally she put it down, went into the kitchen and poured a glass of juice. She was standing in the kitchen, holding the juice in her hand and staring numbly at the wall when the telephone rang again.

"Hello." She held the receiver away from her ear cautiously.

"Kay, it's Bill here," he said shrilly. "I'm calling because Tab just telephoned me. She says that she may have upset you and she thinks that, maybe, I should pick up the pieces."

"I'm not in pieces, Bill." That was only partly true.

"She is really mad, Kay."

"A friend of mine is sick, Bill. Tab thinks I should come home. She...."

"The little policewoman," Bill interrupted. "You were doing some workouts with her. I heard that she got stabbed while on duty."

"How in hell did you know that, Bill?"

"It's in all the papers, Kay."

"I mean," Kay said wearily, "how did you know that I was working out with Mary?"

"Louise...."

"Jesus Christ!" There was a pause, then a hint of pleading crept into Kay's voice. "Bill, I can't come home right now."

"I know, I know," he said quickly. "You are satisfied that the girl is all right. The papers say that she is conscious and alert. The knife didn't hit her heart or her liver or anything like that. I guess that her lung was punctured...."

Kay closed her eyes very tightly. "I thought you were supposed to be picking up the pieces, Bill," she said thickly.

"I'm sorry," he said, suddenly contrite. "I am trying to say that I understand."

"I don't know if you do, Bill."

"Yeah, I do. I was in a big race once. An uncle of mine was sick. I called him and he said not to come. He understood how important the race was."

"You're going to tell me he died, aren't you Bill?"

"Died?" Bill said puzzled. "Hell no. Uncle Alphonse is eighty-four now and as spry as a woodchuck. I won the race. I gave him my trophy. He said it was the best medicine. There are sacrifices in this business."

"Yeah. You've made me feel a lot better, Bill."

"It is better," he insisted. "What good does it do your friend if she has to live with the thought that she has deprived you of your medal? Who would want that?"

"Maybe you could explain that to Tab."

"Jesus, no!" he said emphatically. "I tried that, Kay. She almost took my ear off."

"I'm sorry."

"There is nothing to be sorry about. It's part of my job—to run interference for you."

"You're a good man, Bill Bordeaux."

"The important thing is that you continue your training and avoid letting this thing put a hitch into it. That is enough to

165

concern yourself with. It is all that should be expected."

"Sure."

"You will have the opportunity later to accommodate the other things."

"I hope so."

"I will be in Montreal Friday evening. I will see you then."

"OK."

"In the meantime, I want you to get a good night's sleep and do what Leon says."

"I will."

"It is past midnight now."

"I'll go right to bed, Bill."

Bill said good bye and Kay hung up the receiver. As promised, she went directly to bed. She did not go directly to sleep. She lay there with her hands behind her head, staring at the ceiling and thinking about Mary.

According to the newspapers, Mary had answered a routine call to clear the kids away from Warner's. After the stabbing, the kids had scattered to the winds. The proprietor of Warner's was so scared that he drew the blinds put up the CLOSED sign and huddled in the storeroom until Constable Bulmer came hammering at the door. The proprietor told Constable Bulmer that he had closed early and hadn't seen a thing.

The neighbourhood had failed Mary, Kay thought grimly. Indeed, the hero of the moment was a motorist from Oshawa who summonsed an ambulance and slapped a wad of vaseline gauze from an auto first-aid kit over the sucking chest wound.

Mary, Kay imagined, would forgive the neighbourhood. People down there didn't want contact with the police when there was trouble. Mary understood that. As soon as she was able to return to duty, she would be back on the streets, eager to let her people know that she didn't despise them for leaving her to bleed to death on the sidewalk.

Kay took a deep breath and relaxed. Mary would understand what she was doing too.

* * *

The next day, Leon told her that if she thought what she was doing was right then it was right. He made the statement with the confidence of a man accustomed to reducing complex issues to neat simplicities.

The workouts went on as before.

Bill arrived Friday afternoon. Leon was acting as her spotter in the weight room when he arrived and the housekeeper let him in. He descended upon them with the air of an old pro called in to cap a burning oil well —humbly yet aware of the effect of his presence. Kay watched as Leon hugged Bill and Bill tried to appear indifferent.

"So, I guess you have done a good job, Leon." Bill cast a glance toward Kay who was sitting up on the weight bench. "She looks good."

"She is great." Leon put an arm around Bill again and slapped him on the back. "Everything has worked out just perfectly."

"She didn't give you any trouble?" Leon had knocked the bow tie askew. Bill corrected it fussily.

"Of course not. She has discipline."

"For sure. She knows what is necessary."

"Why don't you talk about me as if I'm not here." Kay didn't wait for a response. She stood up and gave Bill a hug. Leon beamed his approval.

"I'll ask Mrs. Hobar to put out some snacks." Leon disappeared up the steps.

"Did Louise come with you?"

"She came with me. She is at the Village."

"Bill," Kay said, disappointed, "why didn't you bring her

167

with you?"

"She needs to settle in. You will see her at the ceremonies on Sunday."

"I'm getting hungry for female companionship. Mrs. Hobar just doesn't do it for me."

"I will ask Louise to brunch on Sunday then. I was going to take you and Leon anyway."

"Good." She looked at him expectantly. "What about Tab?"

"I spoke to her."

"And? When is she coming?"

"She isn't sure." He looked away, uncomfortable. "She told Louise that she would be here for her events."

"Louise doesn't run until next weekend."

"She said that she might have a class to lecture on Monday." Bill cleared his throat. "I didn't press."

"She can cancel that damned class whenever she wants to." Kay tossed her towel aside petulantly. "She's punishing me. I don't need that. I'm an adult. I haven't raided a cookie jar in years."

"Well, I am sure that she will change her mind and be here for Monday. I never thought that she was serious about the class. It was just something for her to say."

"Well, if she expects me to phone and beg her to come, I'm not going to."

"No, there is no point if it is going to aggravate you."

"I'm already aggravated."

"I'm going up to talk to Leon. Go into the shower and plan what you are going to tell me. I want to hear everything about the past two weeks in detail."

"Including the woman I picked up in the bar on Sherbrooke Street ?"

Bill didn't blink an eye.

"I don't need to know about that," he said.

168

"OK."

"Come up when you are ready." Bill started up the stairs. He paused halfway up. "There was no woman in a bar on Sherbrooke Street."

"No, Bill, there was no woman in a bar on Sherbrooke Street." Kay picked up her towel and headed toward the shower. "I'll be up in a minute." She paused, waiting for a response. There was none. Bill had closed the door behind him. Kay pulled her clothes off and stepped into the shower. "Hell," she said, "there should have been."

Chapter 21

Louise had little to say in Leon's presence but afterwards, as Bill drove them to the stadium to prepare for the opening ceremonies, she was full of news. Debbie was in town, staying with friends near The Big O. Her spot on the team had been filled by a husky youngster from UBC.

Mary was making a good recovery in the hospital. Louise had dropped by Pop's on Friday evening and had gotten the whole story from Jean who had been to visit twice.

"Did Tab say anything to you about Mary?"

"Just that she's annoyed with you. But you already know that."

"What do you think?"

"What should I think?"

"I don't know." Kay glanced at Bill. He was pretending not to listen but she knew he was hanging on every word. "I guess I would like to think that not everybody sees me as some kind of ogre."

"I know how you are, Kay. I know that when you're preparing for a race this big there's nothing else."

"Tab should know that too."

"Tab's been really bitchy the last couple of weeks," said Louise, putting the emphasis on the really. "Something's going on between her and Esther. A lovers' quarrel, maybe."

"Really." Kay glanced at Bill again. She could see his ears

pick up another notch. "What do you think it's about?"

"I don't know. I didn't dare ask. She was like a bear when I saw her." Louise started to laugh. "Maybe it's about something that's happened in bed again."

Bill pretended to be concentrating very hard on the traffic. Kay noticed, to her satisfaction, that the tips of his ears were turning red.

"Did you hear that, Bill?"

Bill shook his head as if he had a buzzing noise in his ears but did not acknowledge her.

"So, maybe it's Esther that she's really mad at," Kay said to Louise.

"Don't worry, dear, she's plenty mad at you too. Tab's got plenty of mad to go around this week."

"Cute."

"By the way," Louise said, lowering her voice, "I've met someone."

"Met someone?" Kay paused. "You mean, here at the Village?"

"Here at the Village."

"So, where's she from?"

"Guess."

"Scandinavia. She's one of those tall, blonde Swedes you get so excited about."

"That was last year."

"Not a Swede," Kay murmured. She was watching Bill's eyes in the rear view mirror. "Maybe a German—one of those cool stoics. Raging inferno on the inside."

"No."

"She's Irish. You fell in love with her accent."

"She's from the Bahamas, dear, the Bahamas."

"Oh," Kay nodded with understanding, "a black woman."

"Very."

"Have you slept with her?"

"What do you think?"

"You're getting very bold in your old age, Louise." Kay shook her head. "So, what does she do?"

"She's a sprinter. 200 metres is her specialty."

"That's great."

"I've an invitation to visit her after the Games."

"You work fast, Louise."

"After this, I deserve some time in the Bahamas. When this is over, I'm going to be so tired they'll be scraping me off the infield," Louise said with a sigh. "I should feel tired now but my mind won't believe what my body's telling it. The Village is one giant shot of adrenalin that never ends. The high goes on for hours and hours."

"Sometimes I think I'm tired all the time," Kay murmured. "I'm tired so much that I've forgotten what it's like not to be tired."

Bill's voice rose from the front seat for the first time. "Hey," he said, "you are healthy young athletes. There is no reason for being tired."

"We're just speculating about what it might be like, Bill. When it happens, we want to recognize it and not chalk it up to steroid withdrawl."

"I don't think you should even say that word."

Bill started into a long lecture about steroids. Louise egged him on. Kay sat back and lost herself in the passing scenery.

* * *

The weather forecasters were predicting that the chance of rain was as high as twenty per cent for the opening ceremonies. The organizers were frantic. Kay surveyed the skyline and thought how funny it would be if the dye from the smart red blazers ran into the pristine white slacks.

There was also a substantial chance of rain for the running

172

of the women's marathon the next morning. Some of the runners were nervous about running in the rain. Kay didn't care. She was ready for anything and nothing would stop her now. She grimaced as Bill ran a red light. Well—almost nothing.

* * *

Kay slipped away from the stadium as soon as possible. The opening ceremonies had been modest, she thought, quite in keeping with the image of an unpretentious middle power.

The flame had been delivered to the stadium by two local runners—one white and one black—and was carried up the steps by a young man afflicted with Friedreich's ataxia. A hush had fallen over the crowd as he made his way unsteadily up the steps. The hush, Kay guessed, stemmed less from the sensitivities of the assembled athletes than from the fear that he was about to topple to his death before their eyes.

"He was once a pretty good runner," Bill told Kay as they headed back to the apartment. "I guess that he won some high school meets in the province. I don't think that they should have asked him to light the flame though. What if he had not been able to do it? It would have been a great failure for him for sure."

"Christ, Bill, if he'd toppled off the first step they would have called it heroic," Kay said irritably.

"You're just mad because some members of the team snubbed you."

"I don't give a damn."

Bill shrugged.

"They were embarrassed," he said. "They are trying to prove to everyone what hardships they have, how they need special funding, how to be a world-class athlete they have to work at it twenty-four hours a day. And, there you are, holding down a job every day, working your training around it." Bill blinked in the gathering fog. "Living in a little rabbit house," he continued, "saving all the extra pennies to go to the international races, wearing warm-up suits that are mended over and over."

"I didn't know that you noticed things like that, Bill."

"Sure I notice. In the old days, we were all like that—all the athletes who were amateurs. Nobody had anything. It was a big personal commitment."

Bill pulled the car to a halt in front of the apartment building. He turned off the ignition but made no move to get out of the car.

"Are you coming in, Bill?"

"No." He paused, clearing his throat. "This is the last chance I will have to speak to you before the race," he said. "At least, the last time when it won't be a rush. I just want to say that I am certain that you will win tomorrow."

"Thanks."

"There is no way you can lose. I am confident that our training has been the best. In any event, you are ten per cent better than any of the other runners."

"Only ten per cent?"

He ignored the remark. "You are the best athlete I have ever coached," he said stiffly. "It has been very gratifying."

"Are you trying to tell me that you don't want to coach me anymore?"

"Sure, I will still coach you." His irritation at her flippancy took some of the formality from his tone. "It will not be so intense, that's all. The last four years have had a lot of intensity." He cleared his throat again. "I would say that you are probably the best runner that I will ever coach but I would like to think that that will not be the case."

"It would make for a dull future."

"Maybe I will coach someone as good but probably not better. Still," he shrugged, "to compare runners of different times.... "

"You'll find someone, Bill." Kay regarded him with affec-

174

tionate amusement. "You'll be at a track some day and you'll see a little middle-distance runner who you'll just know would make a great marathoner."

"Maybe."

"Or one of your old cronies will give you a tip about some fast kid in Smooth Rock Falls."

"Sure."

"Who knows? After the Games, they might want you in Eugene. You might get an invitation to go to Eugene, Bill. You know what they have there."

"Sure, I know what they have there. It is a place for off-the-rack runners." He shook his head. "It's too classy for me there, Kay."

"I know, you're just a kid from Shawinigan Falls."

"Sure." He touched the key in the ignition. "I will call you at five-thirty to make sure that you're awake. Some toast with honey, I think. That's all you should eat."

"That's what I usually eat."

"And lots of water."

"Lots of water."

"I will pick you up at seven, then."

"I'll be ready."

She stood and watched as he drove away. Leon's car seemed to sag even closer to the ground than usual.

Poor Bill, she thought, he was like a father marrying off his only daughter. She also sensed that he felt unworthy of her and that made her feel sad. She had neglected to say anything nice to him. Tomorrow—before the race—it would be too late. He would be even more focussed than usual and he wouldn't absorb a thing she said.

The apartment seemed strangely quiet. Kay poured a glass of juice and took it to the bedroom with her.

In less than fifteen hours, it would all be over. Some of the runners had expressed disappointment with the timing of the marathon. They thought that scheduling the race as the opening event was somewhat diminishing. Kay was glad. The Olympic spirit had already affected some of the athletes, giving them a glassy-eyed, unreal look. By the end of the first week, the atmosphere would become increasingly oppressive. A few would feed from it and be sharpened by it. Far more, however, would disintegrate under its pressure.

Kay got into bed, balancing the glass of juice against her abdomen.The weather forecast for the morning was favourable—a pleasant sixty-five with a soft sprinkling of rain. Perfect conditions for a lovely morning stroll through the streets of Montreal. The anticipation of the race made her smile and drove away the irritation she had felt earlier.

Kay drained the juice glass and set it aside. She turned off the light and fell asleep immediately.

Toward dawn, she had a dream. She was running a marathon—a fuzzy grey and white marathon—with the men in the baggy shorts and stiff black shoes. They floated about her in eerie, spectral silence, united in their dignity and in the purity of their purpose.

They ran beside her into the dawn, then faded one by one into the receding mist.

They were phantoms, existing only in the black and white newsreels and in the soul of Bill Bordeaux.

Chapter 22

Bill phoned at five-thirty on the dot. Kay, crawling out of bed, imagined that he had already showered and shaved and was waiting impatiently for the morning paper.

It was just after six when she heard the knock at the door. The toast had just popped up. Kay buttered it sparingly then spread it thick with honey before answering the door.

"Hello." Tab brushed past her, looking sleepy and rather dishevelled.

"What in hell are you doing here?"

"I told you I would come and I did." Tab dropped her suitcase and went straight to the kitchen. She drew some water for the kettle and placed it on the stove.

Kay followed her into the kitchen, a piece of toast in her hand. "There's an electric kettle."

"I prefer this one. You can never be sure if an electric kettle has boiled properly."

Kay leaned against the counter. "So," she said hesitantly, "did you take the train?"

"I drove." Tab opened the canisters on the counter one by one, searching for a tea bag.

"Upper left-hand corner of the cupboard. They've moved them since you were here last."

"Sometimes people change things around. I'll bet they put the tea bags in a different spot every week."

Kay could not believe that she was having this conversation at six a.m. "What did you do with Caesar?" she asked.

"I left him with Marg and Ruby."

"I thought you didn't like their politics."

"Caesar doesn't know anything about politics. He likes Marg and Ruby."

"Smart cat." Kay poured a glass of water and edged toward the kitchen table. "So, what else is new?" There was an awkward pause."How's Mary?"

"Fine," said Tab, her words deliberately clipped. "She's going home tomorrow."

"That soon."

Tab stared at the tea kettle. "She has someone to take care of her," she said.

There was a long silence.

"I know," Kay said finally."That night I called her room, Constable Patricia York answered the phone. She said, 'Toronto General Hospital, Constable Patricia York speaking.' Just like that—you know, the way people who are used to answering official phones answer phones."

"I'm sorry."

Kay shook her head. "It's OK," she said lightly. "Lucky I wasn't in too deep, huh? I sort of had it figured out anyway— her still being in love with her old lover and all that. So," she shrugged, "I figured it would be better if I just butted out."

"I'm still angry," Tab said stubbornly.

"What in hell for!"

"Because you let her down, Kay." Tab turned the kettle off and moved it to the adjacent element with a crash. "You let her down as a friend. Why didn't you go to see her and tell her what you've told me. 'Mary, I know that you love Pat. I'm glad that you have a second chance. I'm still your friend and I care about you very much.' What would it have cost you?"

"She has Pat. She doesn't need me."

"She was a friend, Kay, a nice woman I thought you really liked."

"I did like her." Kay shook her head."I do like her. I like her a lot."

"But you couldn't bring yourself to sacrifice a single day for her. I'll bet you didn't even try to call her again."

"I told you, I didn't want to interfere."

"I don't believe you, Kay." Tab poured some water over her tea bag and began to punch it vigorously."Kay, you're incredibly selfish. You aren't capable of putting anyone else's feelings above your own for a minute."

"Tab!"

"Calling her might have been awkward," Tab continued fiercely."It might have been difficult to know what to say. Tossing off a few jokes would have seemed inappropriate—even to you. It was easier not to call her or go to visit. It was easier not to write a letter or make any personal gesture. Damned it, Kay, you haven't even called Debbie. She feels so out of the picture right now. She would have loved to receive a call from you. But, no, you never thought of calling." Tab paused to catch her breath."When Kay Strachan goes for the medals, the whole world comes to a grinding halt. No one else matters."

"I don't need this, Tab," Kay said unsteadily."Not three hours before my race."

"I can't see why it would make any difference, Kay. Mary was hurt—she almost died—and you wouldn't expend an iota of emotional energy to deal with that. I doubt very much if anything I say will affect your performance in any way."

"You came all the way to Montreal just to deliver this lecture!" Kay cried."Why didn't you just pick up the phone and call? Better still, why didn't you just tell Louise? She has a terrific memory for everything she hears."

179

"I promised you a long time ago that I would be here for the marathon." Tab sat down at the table and began to sip at her tea. She seemed totally deflated.

"Are you going to be on the picket line with Esther and whoever?"

"No." Tab stared at the table. "I was never committed to the protest, Kay. Besides," she added reluctantly, "Esther and I won't be getting together this weekend. We've decided to see each other less often."

"Less often?"

"Infrequently. Perhaps, never."

"Oh."

"I want you to know that our differences have nothing to do with the fact that she asked you to sleep with her."

"She told you about that!"

"Of course."

"And you aren't mad at her for that?"

"Of course not." Tab frowned. "Now, if you had agreed, I would have been angry with you."

"Of course."

"It would have been so totally at odds with your principles, with your sense of loyalty. I would have felt betrayed."

"Why am I always on the wrong side of the old double standard?" Kay shook her head. "So, what happened? Did she put the toothpaste cap on crooked or something?"

Tab bowed her head. "At first when I felt inferior in the relationship, I thought it was just my basic insecurity showing through. Then I realized that I felt inferior through conscious design. Esther needed me to feel inferior. I thought she wanted an equal partner. I was wrong. She had an overwhelming need to dominate. She praised my academic achievements while informing me subtly that she considered them vastly inferior to her own. She patronized my household skills. I've al-

180

ways been very proud of my skills as a manager, Kay. Esther made me feel that my accomplishments in that area were trivial, that she—if she cared to— could outdo me in that area as well. She wouldn't allow me to imagine that I surpassed her in any way, Kay," Tab concluded somberly. "She wouldn't even let me be equal."

"I'm sorry. For her, I am sorry," Kay hastened to add, "She's missed out on something good. You deserve better than that."

"Thank you."

"Do you want me to punch her out for you?"

"I don't want you to commit any act of violence."

"That's too bad. I feel like committing an act of violence right about now."

Tab did not respond. Kay pushed her plate aside and stood up. "I'd better get dressed," she said."Bill will be here any minute now. Do you want him to drop you off at Leon's? Leon's going to follow the route."

"Perhaps I'll watch the race on television."

"Oh." Kay swallowed hard."Well, why not. You'll probably get a better view. Leon's car will probably fall apart anyway."

She went into the bedroom and dressed quickly, putting on the official white singlet and red shorts and pulling on the official red and white track suit. She could hear Bill at the door as she picked up her equipment bag.

"You could come down and go around with Leon," he was saying to Tab as Kay opened the bedroom door.

"I've already asked her, Bill."

Bill was wearing the track suit that had been distributed to the team coaches, and looked as formal as if he were wearing a tuxedo. He turned to her quickly. "Kay, are you ready?"

"Sure. Tab's going to watch the race on television."

Bill took the equipment bag from Kay. "Too bad," he said.

"Leon will get good spots. He's very good at sneaking his car along the back allies. It will be like being in the middle of the race. Why don't you change your mind and come?"

"No thanks, Bill."

Kay turned to Tab as Bill edged her out the door. "Wish me luck."

"Of course she wishes you luck." Bill steered Kay through the door and closed it before Tab could say a word.

* * *

Kay rehearsed the course in her mind as she waited for the starting gun—a lap around the Olympic Stadium track, St. Zotique, Rosemont, St. Joseph's, Sherbrooke, De Maisonneuve, past Place Ville-Marie, a ridiculous loop just beyond the CBC building before doubling back on Sherbrooke to the Stadium. It was a somewhat bastardized version of the Montreal International Marathon run backwards. The officials, in their wisdom, had decided that it would be good for the Olympics to run the race through downtown Montreal.

The other medal favourites avoided her gaze. Williams of Britain seemed lost in her own thoughts. Thomas was talking to a fellow Aussie. The three Americans bunched tightly together like football players in a huddle. One of them—Westerholme—was considered a dark horse. Rumour had it that she intended to go out fast and attempt to duplicate her feat in the Greater London.

Kay didn't know Westerholme. She knew Ekomoto, the Japanese runner, and Tenari, the tiny Italian. Ekomoto was older and had not improved on her times significantly in recent years. Tenari was young and vastly improved. She had come out of nowhere a year ago to win the Stockholm marathon and qualify for her national team.

The other two Canadians, Kay imagined, would do well to finish. Neither had competed in a major race before and a major marathon was vastly different than the average 26.2 miles. Kipkie looked as impassive as she had the day of the National Capital. But, when Kay looked at Pasderka, the youngster smiled and Kay, feeling charitable, smiled back.

The stadium was packed as the runners moved into the opening lap. The spectators would stay on to watch the race on the scoreboard screen and greet their return. Kay heard her name in periodic bursts from the stands as she circled the track in the middle of the pack of sixty-three runners. Some fans yelled Kay and others yelled Strachan. Others waved Canadian flags in her direction. She knew that Louise and Debbie were in the stands. She finally spotted them in the middle of a contingent of Canadian Olympians in red and white track suits. Louise was waving furiously. Debbie made an obscene gesture. Kay wanted to stop and double over in laughter but the pack was tight and she had to pay attention. She was glad when they left the stadium at last and poured out onto the street, headed for St. Zotique three kilometres away.

On the track, it had been difficult to see what was going on at the head of the pack but as the runners spread out Kay could see the American, Westerholme, in the lead. Four other runners had gone with her at a suicidal pace. Kay calculated that they were setting a 2:22 pace and she expected they would slow once the rush from the stadium crowd dissipated.

The object of the race, for the first six miles, was to get the knots out and establish a rhythm. From that point until about the twenty-mile mark, it was a matter of holding pace. The real race began at the twenty-mile mark.

By the end of St. Zotique, the pack had broken even further. At Rosemont, three of the runners who had gone out with Westerholme dropped back. Only a Danish runner stayed with the American, matching her stride for stride. Kay found herself in the middle of a tight pack of eight runners who had put about fifty yards between themselves and the rest of the field. She took advantage of a water stop to move to the outside of the group. Thomas missed the water stop too and moved out at her elbow. Kay was now at the front of the second pack with Tenari moving up just off her right shoulder.

As they turned onto St. Joseph's, the Danish runner who had gone out with Westerholme dropped back and was eaten up by the pack.

"Do you know how fast we are going?" Tenari's broken accent rose from just behind Kay's right ear.

"Sure"

"We are just better than a 2:24 pace. She has forty-five seconds on us."

"I know."

Kay was tempted to suggest to Tenari that she was talking too much and should save her breath. She decided instead to obey her own injunction. Tenari was getting nervous. She was itching to go after Westerholme who was just visible in the distance, three hundred yards away. Still, she didn't make a move. Smart girl, Kay thought, to stay where the real action was taking place.

As they turned onto Sherbrooke, just beyond the halfway mark, Thomas was getting anxious too.

"Want to go with her?"

"No."

At Sherbrooke and along De Maisonneuve, Kay suddenly became aware of the crowds which were becoming larger and more vocal. People were shouting at her. Kay couldn't hear the words but she sensed the anxiety in their tone. Westerholme seemed a long way away to them. They had seen her and she looked strong.

Kay blocked out the crowd. The noise seemed to dissipate as they passed Place Ville-Marie. Actually, the lines of spectators were getting thicker and noisier. Thomas muttered something under her breath but Kay didn't hear her. She had established an easy rhythm early on and it had not deserted her. She concentrated on her form, making sure that her footplant remained constant and her arm swing fluid.

Just past Place Ville-Marie, Tenari—to everyone's surprise —threw in a surge. It was a short surge and singularly ineffective. Shortly, she fell back to Kay's shoulder. Thomas had not budged an inch.

At thirty kilometres Kay sensed that Westerholme was coming back. She waited until they entered the loop past the CBC building to throw in her first surge. It was a strong five hundred-yard effort.

The result was better than she had expected. When she emerged from the loop, she had gained almost two hundred yards on Westerholme and had put fifty yards between herself and the rest of the pack—with the exception of Thomas who went with her, floating at her left shoulder.

"She's coming back." Kay caught a strong note of relief in Thomas's voice.

Westerholme hung onto a dwindling lead for the next three kilometres. Just before Place Ville-Marie, Kay noticed the awkward movement in the American's left foot. Her arms were dropping and she was hunching her shoulders as if to rid herself of a cramp.

At Place Ville-Marie—with the noise of the crowd once again in her consciousness—Kay passed Westerholme. She didn't look back to see what had happened to the American but, two hundred yards further on, she could hear people in the crowd shouting Tenari's name and flashing fingers and quickly scribbled signs. They were trying to tell her that, apart from Thomas, her only rival was Tenari, fifty yards behind.

Thomas gave no indication that she was faltering. Neither

185

did she hint that she might surge. She hung beside Kay like a shadow. They seemed to breath in unison.

They were back on Sherbrooke, heading home with just six kilometres to go. Kay decided to throw in a short surge—just over three hundred yards. Thomas, reading her mind, was with her from the first step. She surged again with four kilometres remaining. Thomas picked up the pace instantly. It was another short surge.

With two kilometres to go, Kay sensed the excitement in the mobile unit ahead. The spotter was glancing at his watch and shouting into his headphones, trying in vain to make himself heard above the deafening roar of the crowd.

With less than one and a half kilometres to go, Kay threw in the final surge. Thomas was with her at once. Four hundred yards into the surge, Kay slowed —just perceptibly. Then, suddenly, she took off again. This is where I leave you, baby. She said the words to herself and as she said them she could feel herself pulling away. Thomas was a yard behind, then two yards, then Kay couldn't sense her presence at all.

She heard the roar well before she entered the stadium. She was running, she imagined, the fastest mile she had ever run in marathon competition. As she made the final turn of the stadium track, she could see her nearest rival enter the stadium. It wasn't Thomas. It was Tenari. They would tell her later that Thomas had lost her stuffings with the second phase of the final surge.

She crossed the finish line in 2:23:10—over a minute ahead of Tenari—with the stadium crowd on its feet in delirium. Tenari crossed the line, struggled momentarily to control her footing, then came over to embrace Kay. Her time of 2:24:30 was a personal best. She clung to Kay babbling something incomprehensible in Italian. Kay was finally rescued by the Italian coach who pushed through the crowd to pluck Tenari from her. She began to search the stands for Bill.

He was standing in the first row, gesturing enthusiastically with both arms and shouting to her in French.

"Bill."

"Kay." He didn't hug her but continued to flail his arms wildly."It was magnificent."

"Come on, Bill," she said teasingly,"you knew we were going to do it. It was just a matter of running the race. Right?"

"Still it was great. It was a very smart race, Kay. It was smart not to go after Westerholme when she hung on so long. I knew she would come back of course but in a race—when you are the one who is running—it is hard sometimes to realize that."

"I knew she would come back."

"It was a great move that you put on Thomas. She thought you were going to give her a little rest and you fooled her." He leaned further across the railing to make himself heard over the roar of the crowd. Pasderka had just entered the stadium."It's amazing what a little trick like that can do to someone in the last mile. If it had been you, Kay, you would have taken that little lapse as an opportunity to charge. But that's why you are where you are—with the gold medal—and she is only third."

"She folded like a cheap suitcase."

"She lacked the courage. She was afraid to try anything on her own. She was counting so much on beating you with a kick. It's great when you can intimidate them."

"Yeah." Kay glanced toward the track. Kipkie had just crossed the finish line. She collapsed in the infield and lay there, writhing in pain.

"They said she had bad abdominal cramps." Bill followed her gaze. "She took electrolyte replacement at the water stops. I guess it was too strong.'"

"Guess so."

"But you have what you wanted," he concluded happily. "It's all been worth it. Everything...."

Louise and Debbie made their way down from the fourth row. They squeezed in front of Bill and gave Kay a couple of giant hugs. "We are ecstatic, Strachan," Louise said excitedly."We are absolutely hoarse from cheering for you. I don't think I've ever been so nervous, Kay. When she was hanging onto you with 2K to go, I bit all of my fingernails off. I shouldn't have worried. I've seen it all before."

Debbie reached out to shake Kay's hand, nearly crushing it. "How's the finger?"

"Forget it." Debbie released Kay's hand, leaving a ridge of white welts."This is your day, Strachan. You were great. If you hadn't won—well—I don't know."

Kay thought that Debbie was about to cry. Someone several rows up threw down a huge Canadian flag. It fell across her shoulders, draping her like a toga. Kay took the opportunity to turn away from the stands. She hoisted the flag into the air and the crowd which had started to settle down broke into thunderous applause.

* * *

Tab was watching the television as they handed Kay the flowers and hung the gold medal around her neck. Kay had a smile on her face but Tab thought that she looked surprisingly tense.

The remaining medals were presented—the silver to Tenari, the bronze to Thomas. Tenari was ecstatic. Thomas stood, worn and lifeless, her eyes fixed on the ground.

They were playing the national anthem. The cameras flickered between the flag and Kay's profile. The strains of the anthem faded and the crowd burst into applause. Kay took a deep breath and turned to the crowd, holding the flowers aloft. The

188

cameras floated a little uncertainly then, suddenly, zoomed in to pick up the button on the collar of Kay's track suit. There was a dead silence in the broadcast booth.

"Mother Nature is a Lesbian," someone muttered finally.

Tab started to cheer, and then she started to cry.

* * *

Tab was in the kitchen when she heard the key turn in the lock. By the time she reached the living room, Kay was standing in the doorway, her hands behind her back. She was wearing the red and white track suit and the gold medal still hung around her neck.

Tab stopped halfway across the living room. "I was proud of you today, Kay," she said, almost shyly.

Kay shrugged modestly. "Well, it wasn't a PR but I guess it was OK."

"You know what I mean. You did something very important for women today."

"I didn't do it for them," Kay said abruptly. "I did it for you," She reached behind her back and thrust the bouquet forward. It was the bouquet from the podium. "And don't say I never gave you flowers."

Tab stepped forward hesitantly and took the bouquet. "Thank you," she said.

Kay looked at the floor. "There's no candy. I didn't have a chance to check out the silver and I haven't rounded up the perfect house yet."

"Kay...."

"I did bring you something." Kay knelt to open her equipment bag. She brought out a large round object wrapped in tissue and handed it to Tab.

"It's a grapefruit," said Tab, puzzled.

"Yeah, I thought we could pretend that it was Tuesday. Hell woman," said Kay, attempting a show of bravado, "I'm trying

189

to say that I want you." She took the grapefruit from Tab and tossed it onto the couch. "I want to share bodies. I'd even like to take a stab at domiciliary and sexual exclusiveness. I'd like to please you. I know it's not in vogue but maybe if I want to it's all right." She paused suddenly and looked at Tab pleadingly."Jesus Christ, Tab, I can't stand here all day, spilling my guts. Say something."

Tab turned and dropped the bouquet gently to the couch. She didn't say anything but put her hands on Kay's shoulders and looked intently into her eyes.

"It'll solve all your problems," Kay continued quickly. "I'm housebroken. I've got papers. Your mother adores me. Your cat tolerates me. You can run off to North Borneo and know that I'm organized. You can write to me and tell me how to clean the oven."

Tab's eyes were solemn. "I want to memorize everything you're saying because I'll probably never hear any of it again—particularly that part about cleaning the oven."

"No?"

"Fifty years from now, I want to remember that you said you would clean the oven."

"Fifty years from now, you won't be able to remember your own name."

"I'll remember the oven." Tab leaned forward and kissed Kay very lightly so that her lips tingled. She stepped back again just far enough to focus on the expression in Kay's eyes. "I think I'm getting butterflies," she said softly.

"Me too."

"Do you think we can go to bed and get through the first twenty minutes without laughing?"

"I don't know."

Tab kissed Kay again and rested one hand lightly against Kay's breast. The caresses tickled and at first Kay was afraid

190

that she would laugh. But, gradually, the kisses got deeper and her heart started to thump and she knew that she wasn't going to laugh after all.

Chapter 23

The letter was in the mailbox when Kay returned from her afternoon run. She burst through the door, tearing the envelope open as she crossed the floor. Caesar trotted along beside her, jumping into her lap as she flopped into Tab's chair. "It's from Tab," she told him. "See?" She waved the envelope under his nose. "You can smell the Javex. North Borneo's probably a whole lot cleaner than it used to be." Kay smoothed the creases from the letter and began to read. Caesar pressed against her arm with a little squeak. "Want me to read it to you? OK." Kay cleared her throat and began to read aloud:

Dear Kay,

"The Dear Caesar is understood."

By the time you get this letter, I will be home in one month. I am scheduled to arrive in Toronto, April sixteenth. I will wire the details prior to departure.

There was a great feast in the village last night, a comemoration of the coming of age of a former queen of the tribe. The highlight of the meal was a huge platter of a small native....

"You don't want to hear that part," Kay told Caesar.

I was not keen about eating it but my interpreter told me that it would be advisable to do so. Therefore, I ate a small piece.

"Just a small piece, Caesar."

I discovered later that to be asked to participate was a great honour. It means that the women of the tribe have accepted me as a sister.

As I told you in my last letter, the women of the tribe do not understand the Western concept of romantic love. Heterosexual experience seems to be limited, rigidly controlled and confined to phases of the moon and physical signs related to the growing season and harvest. It would appear, however, that they have a rudimentary understanding of the relationship between sex and procreation.

The women are extremely reluctant to discuss sexual matters. You will be interested to know, however, that the sexual initiation of young women is performed by the mature women of the tribe. In fact, some aspects of the initiation ceremonies sound suspiciously like those of normal lesbian sex. The interpreter mentioned casually that, occasionally, these practices take place outside the initiation ceremonies.

"She means there are dykes, even in North Borneo, Caesar."

I had a long letter from Mom yesterday. She tells me that you've been asking her a lot of questions about stoves lately. Kay, all you have to do to clean the oven is spray it with Mr. Muscle and let it sit overnight.

"Wait until she sees the new self-cleaning oven we're getting, Caesar."

The tribe loved the pictures you sent of the Oakland 10K. I was very proud to tell them that you are my friend and that you won the race. Run-

*ning is something the women understand. They
hung the picture of you crossing the finish line
on the center pole of the ceremonial hut.*

"Christ," Kay told Caesar, "in fifty years, they'll be offering sacrifices to me or something."

*I'm still in a bit of a quandary, Kay, between an
associate professorship at U of T or a full professorship at York. Since my notes on the Inuit
were published in Dr. Cain's anthology my academic stock seems to have risen considerably.
By the way, I told the tribe that you have a very
important race in Hawaii next month. The tribe
is planning to sacrifice a wild boar in your honour.*

"So, they're already sacrificing things, Caesar."

Caesar looked at Kay and mouthed a silent meow.

"Don't worry," Kay assured him, "it's not one of your species."

*I thought you looked a little thin in the pic-
tures, Kay. Mom mentioned that you may have
lost a pound or two. Kay, I left you a comprehen-
sive meal schedule. Pay attention to it!*

"Remind me to gain three pounds."

*I don't have any more news, Kay. The supply
car will be leaving in a few minutes so I will
have to say good bye. Give Caesar a pat for me.*

I love you. Tab

"She loves us, Caesar."

*PS —I'm going on a ceremonial pigeon hunt to-
morrow.*

"I bet she'll have to eat the things for dinner."

Kay sat for a few minutes holding the letter in her hand. Finally she got up, still holding the letter, and went into the

194

kitchen. The refrigerator was almost empty and smelled stale.

"She's right," she told Caesar who had followed her into the room. "She said I'd live like a clam while she was away."

She took out the milk and poured some into a glass, feeling suddenly lonely and depressed. She stood for a moment at the kitchen window, looking at the waning light of the late winter afternoon. The church bells in the distance struck four. Caesar moped at her feet. Kay reached down to pick him up. "Hey," she said, brightening, "why don't we have dinner with Ma? She said she had nothing to do tonight. We could take a pizza. What do you say?"

Caesar wrapped his arms around her neck and started to purr.

The End

Judith Alguire lives and writes in southeastern Ontario, Canada. She is keenly interested in animal welfare issues and has a hopeless passion for sports of all kinds. Her personal sport is running which she does with enthusiasm.

Other Titles Available
Order from New Victoria Publishers, P.O. Box 27, Norwich, Vt. 05055

Lesbian Stages by Sarah Dreher (9.95)
Five of Sarah Dreher's wonderfully poignant and funny plays. "The Dreher style is a blend of warmth, droll one-liners, casual repartee, sly observation and passionate, wrenchingly honest explorations of women coming to terms with their personal histories and with their relationships to other women." —*Amherst Bulletin*

Gray Magic by Sarah Dreher (8.95)
A peaceful vacation with Stoner's friend Stell turns frightening when Stell falls ill with a mysterious disease and Stoner finds herself an unwitting combatant in the great struggle between the Hopi Spirits of good and evil.

Something Shady by Sarah Dreher ($8.95)
Travel agent/detective Stoner McTavish becomes an inmate in a suspicious rest home on the coast of Maine to rescue a missing nurse.

Stoner McTavish by Sarah Dreher (7.95)
The original Stoner McTavish mystery introduces psychic Aunt Hermione, practical partner Marylou, and Stoner herself, who goes off to the Grand Tetons to rescue dream lover Gwen.

Look Under the Hawthorn by Ellen Frye (7.95)
A stonedyke from the mountains of Vermont, Edie Cafferty, sets off to search for her long lost daughter and, on the way, meets Anabelle, an unpredictable jazz pianist looking for her birth mother.

Runway at Eland Springs by ReBecca Beguín (7.95)
Anna, a pilot carrying supplies and people into the African bush, finds herself in conflict when she agrees to scout and fly supplies for a big game hunter. She turns to Jilu, the woman who runs a safari camp at Eland Springs, for love and support.

Promise of the Rose Stone by Claudia McKay (7.95)
Mountain warrior Isa goes to the Federation to confront its rulers for her people. She is banished to the women's compound in the living satellite, Olyeve, where she and her lover, Cleothe, plan an escape.

Morgan Calabresé; The Movie by N.Leigh Dunlap (5.95)
Some of the funniest comic strips to come out of the Lesbian/Feminist press. Lesbian and gay politics, relationships, life's changes, and softball as seen through the eyes of Morgan Calabresé.

Radical Feminists of Heterodoxy by Judith Schwarz (8.95)
Revised edition of the history of Heterodoxy, the club for unorthodox women that flourished in Greenwich Village from 1914 until the 1940s. It included many of the best known writers, actresses, and other professional women, as well as members of the suffrage movement. Many original photos and cartoons.